LOVE ISN'T ALWAYS EASY . . .

Bird had gone to bed worried about whether Lem actually went where he'd said he was going, and angry at her husband for choosing to volunteer rather than spending some time with her—but now she was ready to fight for him.

Nobody was coming between her and her man, not even her well-meaning but off-the-wall sister. Not even her favorite sister, so Teri had better get out of their business!

She'd just rock her man's world when he got home, fix whatever was wrong between them, and go about their business. Lem had issues, that was true. But she still loved him, and just because they were the youngest didn't mean they always had to take everybody's advice!

Based on the television series *Soul Food*.
Based upon the characters created for the
motion picture, *Soul Food*, written by

GEORGE TILLMAN, JR.

soulfood

FOR BETTER, FOR WORSE

LESLIE ESDAILE

**writing as
LESLIE E. BANKS**

POCKET BOOKS
New York   London   Toronto   Sydney   Singapore

The sale of this book without its cover is unauthorized. If you purchased this book without a cover, you should be aware that it was reported to the publisher as "unsold and destroyed." Neither the author nor the publisher has received payment for the sale of this "stripped book."

This book is a work of fiction. Names, characters, places and incidents are products of the author's imagination or are used fictitiously. Any resemblance to actual events or locales or persons, living or dead, is entirely coincidental.

An *Original* Publication of POCKET BOOKS

POCKET BOOKS, a division of Simon & Schuster, Inc.
1230 Avenue of the Americas, New York, NY 10020

Copyright © 2002 by Paramount Pictures Corporation

All rights reserved, including the right to reproduce this book or portions thereof in any form whatsoever. For information address Pocket Books, 1230 Avenue of the Americas, New York, NY 10020

ISBN: 0-7434-5739-0

First Pocket Books printing October 2002

10 9 8 7 6 5 4 3 2 1

POCKET and colophon are registered trademarks of Simon & Schuster, Inc.

For information regarding special discounts for bulk purchases, please contact Simon & Schuster Special Sales at 1-800-456-6798 or business@simonandschuster.com

Cover photo by Matthew Jordan Smith

Printed in the U.S.A.

FOR BETTER, FOR WORSE

prologue

bird Van Adams stood behind her client, testing the curling iron and listening to the idle chatter zigzagging through her salon. As she waited for the iron to heat, she moved freeze spritz and a jar of brown gel nearer, by the bank of quarter-inch to three-inch rounds.

Although she automatically participated in the happy banter within Cut It Up, part of her brain was a million miles away. Where was her husband?

After a long stretch of peace, the years of drama with Lem felt like they were beginning again. She loved him and he was a good father, but hadn't they been down this road before? All those arguments and household tension, only to find out that he hadn't been with another woman, or wasn't somewhere shaky. She still had a few trust issues to hurdle, and that had always been the center of any conflict with the man she dearly loved.

Tonight, she'd make Lem's evening special and would squash all the drama between them. After she rocked his world, maybe he'd think twice about going off to some Community Center every Wednesday night. That's all they needed to do—get back to the basics.

Bird picked up the heated curling iron and sectioned off her client's hair. There had been enough icy attitude about Lem's new volunteering efforts; it was time to turn up the heat in their relationship again. They needed to spend some time together as a family, too—her, Lem, and their baby boy, Jay. Tonight, she would banish any negative thoughts about her man. She had a long-overdue surprise for her husband, from Victoria's Secret.

She held the thin strand of her client's new weave between two fingers, and slid the iron down it to produce a curl. Her mind returned to the surprise she was planning, and she didn't realize how long she'd been lost in thought until she saw smoke coming from the curl. Oh, no! *Lord have mercy.*

Alarm swept through her, though she tried to appear calm. Whew! The curl was almost fried, but no big deal. It could be fixed. Luckily, she'd caught her mistake before it was too late. Bird almost laughed as she picked up another strand of nylon weave. She *had* to get her mind off how much she was missing her man.

Almost twelve weeks of Lem being out at nights volunteering for a Community Center, when he had never done anything like that before, was wearing her out. Men had backward logic. They fixed one minor problem by creating a bigger problem than the one they were trying to fix in the first place! If he'd wanted her to give him more attention, or to tighten their bond, he could have simply stayed home at night. He didn't need to go off and do some altruistic thing to get her to recognize his worth. Men were so crazy.

Bird quickly dropped the second curl, which was also beginning to smoke, and glanced at her customer. Shoot! She'd almost torched the sister's nylon again. That would have been a royal pain in the butt, because then she'd have to unglue the messed-up sections and reapply two new ones. This was her last head for the evening, and she had to get home. She had a special dinner to make, a dessert to prepare, had to get her son to sleep so that she and Lem could—

"Girl, you're puttin' a lotta heat on those curls, don't you think?"

Bird jumped, then swiftly covered. "You want it to hold, or do you want to be back in here tomorrow?"

"You're right," her client said with a laugh, relaxing. "It ain't like you're burning up my stuff. Go ahead, Miss Bird—do your thing."

"Thank you," Bird replied with a sheepish grin. "I *am* the best. That's why you all come here and fight for an appointment in my chair."

"Then beat this head like you know how, Sis. I've got a hot date tonight and need to be slammin' for this one. Go ahead and work your magic."

Bird smiled. She could relate. She had a fun evening of her own planned, and had to stop rushing.

Working with renewed fervor, Bird began styling her client's hair. It was a hairdo that she could do in her sleep, which was a blessing. Getting any real rest at night had become impossible. Lem had been so distracted and so tired lately. Too tired with working his day gig at Chadway Towing, and then running around for the Community Center at night, to really *do* anything. She hoped his claim of volunteering was on the up-and-up. Not knowing for sure what he was really doing was making her nerves fray, just like the strand of auburn weave she'd just dropped. But a little one-on-one affection ought to fix that.

one

Lem Van Adams had worked for twelve weeks to be ready for his appointment with the Community Development Center's small-business coaching squad. Twelve long weeks of sitting in Wednesday night classes working on his dream, making up excuses to his wife about where he'd been, trying to get Bird to trust that he wasn't the same man who'd done her wrong in the past. But that had always been the issue: trying to get the family to see that, this time, he'd really changed.

Right now, during the short lunch break from his tow truck gig, he had to prove it to his tough entrepreneurial instructors—and ultimately to a bank. Lem could feel perspiration dampening his undershirt and threatening to seep through to his Chadway Towing uniform.

This whole thing was serious stress. His classmates had warned him to be ready to deal. The instructors had told him to be prepared to put away all defensiveness, and to stand and take whatever they told him like a man. This coaching session was for his benefit, and they weren't there to pull any punches. They were there to kick his ass, polish his proposal, and ask all the hard questions that would be hurled at him by the banks. It was like getting a prizefighter ready for a major bout. He could dig it, but sitting and waiting, and watching other people come out of the boardroom with their tails between their legs, was messing with him. He'd have preferred a clean kill—two shots in the back of the head. This dangling by the end of a thread. . . . Damn!

As Lem watched his fellow classmates leave their one-on-ones, their expressions told him that when it was his turn, it would be more like an intervention—an in-your-face, break-your-balls type of deal. He saw one lady, who was normally tough in class, slip out of the door, take a deep breath, and wipe tears from her eyes. They weren't playing in there.

When his turn came, he sucked it up, stood, and strolled into the room, trying to appear nonchalant. Then he waited as the consultants opened their thick files and began reading in silence. He could hear the clock tick on the wall, it was so quiet. He kept his gaze on the tops of their heads as they reviewed his entire life and his dreams on paper.

"Mr. Van Adams, this is a fabulous project!" Iola Carter stood and leaned across the table to shake Lem's hand. "This concept can work, do you hear me? There's no competition in the immediate vicinity, your demographic profile of the target market is tight, and your multiple revenue streams are a good hedge against risk."

Stunned, he accepted Iola Carter's firm handshake. Her brilliant smile and warmth registered within the marrow of his bones. This efficient, classy sister, who reminded him so much of his sister-in-law, Teri, with her expensive suits, flawless corporate makeup on a high-yellow complexion, and understated jewelry, had just accepted him in his own right. His marketing coach, a near clone of the critical Teri Joseph, saw something in him. A smile eased its way across his face.

Iola Carter slid a proposal across the desk at him from her file.

"Thanks, coach. Couldn't have done it without you." A sense of pride swept through Lem as he studied the bound, typed, and graphically highlighted proposal that this angel of knowledge and mercy had just dropped on him. They had actually gone in and spruced up what he'd given them earlier. Deep.

"This looks really good," Lem murmured, in awe of how the center had taken his handwritten chicken scratch and transformed it into a Wall Street wizard's report. "Damn."

"Presentation is everything, Lem. Right? It's all in the packaging. But you gave us something solid to work with."

At the moment he could only chuckle as he nodded, and then he glanced at the other coaches around the table for affirmation.

"Well, last week I told you we might have a surprise for our star student, too," Iola added with a wink. "Seems as though the center has really taken you on as a model success story. I'd like you to meet Bruce Pulaski, who has joined us. He's a University of Chicago grad, and he is putting in some community service hours on behalf of the architectural firm where he's just taken a new job. He was excited about sinking his teeth into a real project, and he's read your business plan."

She then smoothed the front of her long taupe jacket and adjusted her pearls, but she never stopped smiling. "Don't worry. All of our consultants must sign confidentiality statements with regard to client information, and he's got something to show you. Bruce Pulaski, Lem Van Adams."

"It's a pleasure to meet you, Mr. Van Adams," the new consultant said, thrusting his hand forward in a way that made him seem like an excited puppy.

Lem shook the young white male's hand, and then waited. Perhaps it was too many brushes with the system, or maybe it was justifiable paranoia from growing up black in Chicago, but he took his time warming up to this eager new person on the team. A pair of steel-gray eyes held him in an intense gaze. The new man removed his hand from Lem's, raked his fingers through his dark brown hair, and continued to beam at Lem. Okay, so the guy was over-the-top friendly, maybe even nervous about being here, and trying to make a good impression in a room full of heavy-hitter, African-American business coaches. All that aside, what was this kid going to show him?

Pulaski looked like a clean-shaven hippie, wearing baggy painter's pants, a tie-dyed shirt, and Tims. Lem would have sized him up as being barely out of college, even if Iola Carter hadn't let on that some architectural firm was the guy's first job. However, Pulaski shared the same electrified grin that his marketing coach had on her face. They looked like two little kids right before Christmas, and were practically giggling.

"I don't get it," Lem finally admitted, smiling. Their excitement was catching. "What?"

Russell Hampton, the finance coach, was also smiling. Something was definitely up, because Russell was usually very no-nonsense and delivered just the facts. His dark, somber face normally held the analytical intensity of a banker, and brotherman was the coach who delivered bad news to folks in class when their ideas loomed too large. Russell had already taken several chunks out of Lem's ass about his ex-offender record.

Russell cleared his throat and unfastened the second button on his blue, pin-striped suit and leaned forward on his elbows against the long, mahogany boardroom table, making a tent with his fingers. Light from the fluorescent overhead lamps glinted off his clean-shaven head, which matched the color of the table Russell leaned on.

Linda Maxwell, the legal coach, was fidgeting in her chair as though she would levitate from it at any moment. This was not the sister's normal demeanor, either. Then she began fiddling with one of her locks, tucking it behind her ear, and adjusting her silver and amber earring. Her pretty brown eyes twinkled with a secret, and then she winked at him, too.

"Okay, okay, show him," Iola Carter finally said with a laugh, causing Bruce Pulaski to spring from his chair and dash to the back of the room.

The young man hoisted up four white boards that had been leaning against the wall and rushed back to the table. "Check it out, Mr. Van Adams," Pulaski said in an excited rush. He held the boards so the blank sides were facing the group, then suddenly flipped them over like a magician casting a scarf before an enthralled audience.

"I got inspired, see, and I hope you don't mind that I took it upon myself to work on this all weekend, but Ms. Carter explained what you wanted to do. The Shoppes at Van Adams Court," he went on, almost without taking a breath. "I read your plan, drove by the location, and I was like, 'awesome, dude.' Fabulous location, man. The name thing, I just dreamt it up to slot something into the marquee part of the drawings—you can change it, I wasn't trying to presume. But I couldn't shake this project out of my skull, so I started sketching, and voilà. Hope I did your head vision justice. Check it out. The poetry slam and comedy area could be Van Adams Slam Central, to go with the Shoppes at Van Adams Court thing. You see where I'm going. Strong name—you should use it. Play with it, but you have three parts of this project that you've gotta name: the retail area, the after-school area, and the club area."

Bruce slid the white foam boards across the table to Lem one by one. Lem could only gape at the renderings. These drawings were not skeletal blueprints that a person had to wrap their mind around to envision; this was art. Somehow this young architectural artist had been able to enter his brain and convert black-and-white text into the vision held by his soul.

"I thought you guys were only going to do blueprints," Lem whispered. "This is blowing me away."

"Cool." Bruce beamed, pacing back and forth. "Maximum impact. I can get one of the technical guys to walk through the building and give you the bones in blueprint, but first ya gotta see it. If you're pitching to banks, they have to understand the whole concept, and then you can go into details. But you have to see it."

"No doubt," Lem muttered in appreciation as his voice trailed off. His name was on a building that showed a renovated version of his dream. It was even landscaped, swathed with trees and a new paint job on the lower portion. The new signage and classy awnings made him hold his breath for a moment until he remembered to breathe.

On the second board, the young artist gave two perspectives of the retail stores that had been exploded and pulled out to show upscale shops filled with patrons in one view, and an open atrium mall view from an interior angle in the other. The third board had the after-school program, with expanded views of instructors in the tutoring and computer center common area, with some kids gathered in comfortable seating, others at individual desks listening to lessons on tapes, while still more sat in divided classrooms near a small library section within the Van Adams Learning Tree.

But what Pulaski had done with the club section made Lem slowly sit down before his knees gave way.

"How did you know?" Lem's voice came out as a whisper.

"You like it?" Iola Carter rounded the desk. "Just look at it, Lem. We can sell this to any community economic development board. Look at how it turns blight into a revitalized strip, and provides jobs in an area that so desperately needs them. Oh, my God, Bruce, you are all that!"

"Bruce, man," Lem stammered, "they told me I'd probably get some free blueprint work, but I never expected anything like this."

Linda Maxwell was standing now, her fingers gently caressing the edges of the art boards. "This is what we came in here to do, everybody. This is the type of project and student that makes you know it's all worthwhile. Lem Van Adams, you have to do this in our community. You have no choice. I will move heaven and earth and anyone on my Rolodex to help get this project off the ground. Zoning boards, community groups, a few political letters of support to assuage the financing people. You just say it, and this whole office will pull out the stops to help you achieve this. Good work, Pulaski. Welcome to the team."

"I'm glad you all like it," Bruce said with pride. "I could see where he was going in my head, and couldn't turn it loose until I put it down on paper, you know what I mean? Something hits you and you get caught up by it."

"Yeah, I do," Lem agreed with a nod. "Been dreaming about doing something like this for years—until I came here, I just didn't know how to begin."

"The cash flows make sense, the asking price of the building makes sense, and all of the projections point to this being a good idea," Russell remarked with an easy tone. "We should invite the sellers to his graduation, because it's a small, family-owned property that—"

"No, no, no no no! Are you insane?" Iola Carter paced in a circle.

"We have to address Van Adams's record. I hate to throw cold water on all this enthusiasm, but if we don't deal with it now, it will come back to haunt us," Russell said.

Frustration rekindled itself as Lem thought about how to respond. "Yeah, okay," he said after a moment, feeling defensive as he felt his dream begin to evaporate right before his eyes.

"Why should a bank or any other financial institution trust you—after you did something untrustworthy enough to get yourself locked up?"

Russell's question stabbed at a tender wound. The room went still and all positive vibes disappeared.

"Because I have paid my debt to society, for one," Lem said in an even tone. He held his emotions in check as he spoke, his gaze intense on Hampton. "For two, I have demonstrated by my ability to singlehandedly turn around a complex family operation, gain the management skills to run a store, make it profitable, and employ people from the neighborhood—J&H Grocery. My wife and I, as marital partners, own a salon; we have a significant stake in a family property—which covers more than three quarters of the requested amount of financing—and cash in the bank. All from legitimate, trackable sources. Any additional questions?"

Lem stared at Russell Hampton, and their gazes locked in a silent struggle. Then Russell threw him off balance—he smiled.

"Like a pro, Lem. Like a pro. When they ask those same questions during your presentation, you answer them just like you answered me. But lose the edge in your voice. Understood?"

Lem let his breath out quietly and slowly so the coaches couldn't see it. Damn, they weren't playing. While he appreciated their testing him, and Russell taking the role as devil's advocate, answering that one question never got easy. He relaxed and tried to settle back into his chair, clutching what remained of his dignity firmly in his mind. "Cool." What else could he say?

The room erupted as the consultants now argued, talked about him in the third person, and threw around acronyms and terms that he vaguely remembered from class. He thoroughly got the concepts, but it was hard to keep up the mental translation to the new vocabulary he'd just learned. It was also like being a dead man with people talking about him over his grave. The project had life and soul, and strangely he felt like he was just a lifeless body in the room.

Their intense comments zapped across the table like an out-of-control arcade game. Each time he tried to get a word in edgewise, another consultant would slap him with facts about his creditworthiness, his past. Yet, just as he was about to flare up in anger, another would soothe his battered ego by telling him how fantastic a person he was—someone worth their time, energy, and risk. The tension was exhausting. Spikes of adrenaline shot through him as though he were on a wild emotional roller coaster. Then they stopped, smiled, and stared at him.

"Okay, then," the finance coach finally said, rubbing his chin, "the board should be at the graduation to see this presentation and to be convinced that they should step in at this level. Van Adams is one of the top five in the class, if not number one—his idea is the best. He came here with more resources than most. Unlike many of the students who come through here, he also did the real research on his own, putting his nose to the grindstone. I'm willing to push him in front of our board—his one and only significant blemish notwithstanding."

Lem looked around the room as the pace and pressure kicked up a notch.

"Done," Iola said with confidence. "I know they'll want this to happen. It just makes too much sense." She clicked the button on the wall to lower a screen and picked up a remote control, firing up Power Point. "Which is why I had our intern, Zelda, in here all day playing with this."

"Everything else said and done, though, I take it you seriously like the renderings." Bruce laughed, leaning across the table to shake Lem's hand again.

Lem held the palm within his for a moment longer than before. "It's all that, as the lady said, and I'm down for whatever."

The two exchanged a nod of appreciation, then Bruce laughed again and pounded Lem's fist. "Cool."

"I'll work the board with Iola," Linda offered, rallying to the challenge, "and Russell, just stand by to help them make financial sense of it for the organization. It's in line with our mission statement, so the acquisition shouldn't be an issue. What's going to be problematic for us as a nonprofit organization is giving him a lease-to-own deal with a one-year stay on the mortgage payments while renovations are under way, if we can't get the sellers to hold the mortgage for him."

Iola Carter nodded and let her breath out slowly. "The board *will* fuss that they are a nonprofit, yada, yada, yada, and can't pay the mortgage for a year while Van Adams gets the building in shape—but let me work that."

"The sellers could potentially hold the mortgage without payments beginning for six months to a year under a structured agreement, since they're only paying property taxes on it now. No doubt the mortgage was paid off on it years ago, and our title search shows there are no liens. One way or another, the site is golden," Linda Maxwell said.

Lem's coaches' comments continued to ricochet and fly by him like rapid gunfire. In truth, he wasn't listening to them that closely any longer. His mind was focused on two things: explaining all this to Bird, and getting around his record. He got most of what they were saying as his mind dodged behind his own inner thoughts and out again to the conversation around the table. He knew the crux of what was being discussed was how to bankroll the deal, who he'd ultimately pay on a monthly basis, but the political dynamics about the nonprofit versus the seller was something he'd have to sit down with a coach one-on-one about. For now, he was feeling their vibe, which was mostly positive, intense, and about supporting him. That much he got from just knowing people.

Iola Carter nodded, and finally sat down with the remote control in her hand. "That should mean the Department of Commerce and Community Affairs has some funding we can tap, given that we are a 504 certified development corp. This beaut is only going for one-fifty in its current condition."

"I'm not concerned about our board," Russell hedged. "I want to be sure that we can leverage the two-fifty required for the renovations. He's going to need ten to twenty percent equity in this deal and the Small Business Administration 7a program lenders might not want to—"

"We'll talk about that later," Iola cut in. "Let's go over the Power Point first. Our client is obviously worn out; I can see it on his face. It's a lot to take in, and he has passed the test. We knew what we were working with from his initial intake interview, and we accepted him into our program anyway. We'll deal with these background issues during the week. Good job, Bruce. Great job, Mr. Van Adams."

Iola Carter's hand covered Lem's and briefly squeezed it in support. She'd been the one to whom he'd opened up, really told what he wanted to do in life, and now she'd come to his rescue to block any further damage to his pride. She was in his corner, and was pumping up his fatigued spirit. It was all good. Lem gave her a nod to convey the thanks he was too emotionally exhausted to utter. She nodded back, obviously receiving the mental telepathy. His shoulders dropped two inches in relief. He was blessed.

"Let's not have this student who worked so hard, who has so much promise and a solid business background, get snowed under by all the financial hypothetical situations at this juncture. We're going to do our best to work it out. Like my grandma used to say, there ain't no such word as *can't*." Again, Iola Carter backed off the pit bulls at the table. That was power.

Lem knew in his heart that it would be a stretch to get anyone to fund an ex-con. But the fact that this team fought for him, pumped him up, and made him try to go for it nonetheless, made all the difference in the world. He was relieved that there was such a committed group of individuals who thought his dream was worth going out on a limb for. It was a Hail-Mary proposal, as Russell had once said, but the team was fighting for him regardless. That counted for a lot.

When Iola began the Power Point presentation, Lem's gaze adhered to his technology-transformed, multicolored company pitch. Bold hues flashed up on the screen as the marketing coach talked him through the bulleted points he'd need to familiarize himself with to sell himself and his dream.

Combined voices and affirmations, akin to the inspiration a person could receive from an intense church choir, made him swallow hard with emotion. Never in his life had he felt so alive, so accepted, so supported by any group of people so positive, and this feeling of empowerment was coming from this tiny circle of probably underpaid experts who gave up lunch hours and worked nights to help nobody become somebody.

The colors on the screen blurred as sudden moisture filled Lem's eyes and burned away. People with education and respectable professions were egging him on, telling him he could do this, how possible it all was. It reminded him of something Hardy Lester, the old half-owner of J&H Grocery, once said: "Don't never let nobody tell you what you can't be or do."

If this was what having a chance meant, if this was what being viewed as an equal felt like, if this was what being your own man could do, then he'd die trying to hold on to this dream—if not for himself, then for his son. Lem's gaze remained fastened to the screen as Iola Carter flipped each slide, the name Van Adams boldly at the top of each one. His son, Jeremiah, would have a chance to feel like this one day if he could get it right, and maybe Jay would even be able to expand what his father had built.

There were simply no words. His marketing coach and primary evening instructor had given him the thumbs-up. His legal coach was committed to move hell and high water to support him. A young white boy who was just out of college, who didn't ask about his background and didn't know him, was excited enough to understand what he dreamed of. His finance coach had applauded his idea as sound, and the conservative warning in Russell's voice no longer rattled him. Russell Hampton was clearly impressed by the work he'd done, the numbers he'd crunched during his lunch breaks or while sitting in the truck waiting on a tow call. If nobody else did, Russell knew the depth of research he'd committed himself to, dropping in and out of libraries during the day and on the weekends. Russell knew what he was up against, as a man. That's why the brother wouldn't let him forget and be lulled into some false sense of security. A true brother didn't let another brother go out like that, believing in fairy tales. That was cool of Russell.

Lem felt validated by their support. Bird would be so proud.

He couldn't wait to get home to his wife.

two

"Hey, baby, you going to that Center tonight, or you gonna eat with me and Jay?"

"With you, but then I need to make a last run for Kenny." He watched Bird walk toward him from the kitchen with their son in her arms. Skintight jeans hugged her petite, curvaceous form. He had to admit that his wife looked beautiful in that shiny rust-colored sweater, which perfectly matched the hue of her pixie haircut and clung to her torso like skin. He loved the way her mischievous smile gave off a thousand watts against her cocoa skin. When he finally got his business rolling, she'd really light up in her new salon. Keeping the surprise under wraps was killing him.

"Why don't you have to go to the Community Center after you make the tow run for Kenny? I thought you had two more weeks—or did you quit?"

Absorbing the sight of her made him hold in check what would have been an irate response. Weeks of no play and crazy arguments had a way of mellowing a brother. All he wanted was peace. He had enough on his mind.

"No," he murmured. "Didn't quit. Ran by there earlier today on a late lunch break."

Bird raised an eyebrow, but when his son reached for him and smiled, relaxation eased back into Lem's muscles. He leaned down and pecked Bird on her lips, noticing that she lingered for a moment as though savoring their kiss before giving him the baby.

"I told those people I'd do the time," he said gently. "Only got two more weeks till the class graduates, and I gotta keep my promise to help out with the young brothers. Wouldn't be right to pull out this late in the game." He still didn't dare tell her the real reason he went to the Center.

Kissing his son and tickling the child's neck with his nose, making the baby laugh, he glanced at Bird from the corner of his eye. "I'm gonna need to scoff up dinner, then jet. Cool? You know our brother-in-law is trying to squeeze every nickel out of the day and night, so I'm still technically at work right now. Ain't even clocked out yet. Wanted to see y'all, 'cause it might be late when I get in."

Bird sucked her teeth. "I thought you might come home, take a shower, and stay home tonight."

"I had to work a longer shift today. After I'm done with my commitment at the Center, then I'll be home more regular hours. Fair?"

He smiled, knowing why she wanted him to take a shower. He'd make it up to her tonight.

"All right," Bird sighed, sashaying ahead of him toward the kitchen. "Just miss you, is all. With me working crazy hours at the salon until I get a new stylist to fill an empty chair, and you working like a bulldog for Kenny, and adding on this volunteer community thing out of the blue, I hardly get to see my husband anymore."

He helped his son into the high chair and took a seat across from him at the kitchen table. Although he didn't say it to Bird, he liked that she missed him the way he missed her. It meant that a truce was in the offing, and they could quash the arguments that had cropped up about his wanting to volunteer in the first place.

Lem pushed back from the table and stretched his legs, working the knots out of his shoulders while his baby boy tried to feed himself, reveling in the texture of mashed potatoes that his mother had set before him. Not a year old and his boy was already trying to handle some things. Yeah, just like his daddy.

Jay's dark, intense eyes were riveted to his happy task, and his smooth brown face was crusted with white potato gunk. His boy needed a haircut badly. Jay's curly Afro looked like Don King had styled it, adding mashed potato spikes for an extreme punk vibe. Lem chuckled as he watched the delighted child gurgle while the food squished between his tiny fingers. He wished his own goals were so simple and easy to hold in his hands.

"I don't see why missing one meeting over there at that Community Center would have been such a big deal. If you hadn't taken time off from the job earlier today, you could have come straight home. We haven't spent any quality time together in a while—*like weeks.*"

Lem felt a smile slide onto his face. Yeah, she was feeling it, too. Which made him not take offense at her complaint.

" 'Cause I gave 'em my word, Bird." He'd made sure that his tone was more like a plea than a rough statement. He wanted to keep the peace, have her be in the same state of mind when he got back home. Now was not the time to get into a struggle with his wife, and the last thing he wanted was to walk out of the house during an argument.

"You gave me your word, too, that we wouldn't wind up like some old married couple. We haven't even hit thirty yet, and it's been *a while* since I've seen you—at night, you know what I mean? But I guess you haven't noticed."

Why couldn't women understand that when a brother was all messed up in the head thinking about things, sometimes getting some wasn't a priority? But she had a point. It had been a few weeks. The arguing about his time hadn't helped. Not to mention, she looked good in those jeans. Smelled great when he'd kissed her. His wife was making the goal to leave very hard right now. He chuckled as he watched her pout. She knew what she was doing. He was sure of that when she smiled, too. Bird was a trip.

"What if you came to the class graduation?" He asked the question in an offhanded manner. The logistics could be tricky. Bird might flip when she found out that he was actually *in the class,* not just a street-type reality instructor. She might flip even more when she learned what he'd been up to.

Lem chuckled more deeply as she continued to stare at him with one of her "Bird looks" that said "pulleeze" without words. He should have thought it through before asking her to go down there. Trying to start a business on his own, with no Joseph Chadway family support, without getting everyone's buy-in and permission to proceed, and possibly quitting his job with Kenny to do it, was a potentially explosive dynamic. Maybe that's why he loved the concept so. This time he didn't have to ask "Mother, may I?" of any of them.

"You want me to come down there?" Bird stood in front of the stove, her gaze trained on him while she held his half-filled plate of food in her hand.

"Yeah," he replied casually. "We've been passing like ships in the night, like you said. So maybe we could do something together . . . kill two birds with one stone. You could meet the people down there, see the Center firsthand, and afterward we could go to dinner, maybe roll over to Groove Theory for a drink and a little dancing. Maybe Maxine would watch Jay?"

"Well, if I did come down that night, you'd definitely have to get a shower and change before we went." She smiled.

"I'll take that as a yes to my invitation. And yeah, I'll be suited down."

"A suit? Why not your fly—"

"It's a graduation, Bird. We gotta dress like we're going to church. Conservative."

"Uhmmm. So, we'll have to change twice, because I'm not bouncin' into Groove Theory wearing church clothes, okaaay?"

"If that's what you want to do, fine. But I can't be late that night."

"You got all mad when I called down there before, so what's up now?" She tilted her head to the side, and offered him a sassy pout. "Now I can come down to your volunteer thing?"

He smiled. In a way, he *was* volunteering, with a class that was learning about business principles. He just hadn't let on that he was a student in those classes, instead of a guy who knew how to run a store and was helping out with the teaching. But since Bird hadn't asked for more details, he hadn't offered them.

"That's because you were checking up on me. But this is different," he murmured as he stood to walk toward her and placed a kiss against her neck, and then nipped it.

"Oh," she said with a giggle, keeping her face close to his. "How so?"

"This is an invitation."

"Oh, I see. An invitation is different."

"Way," he replied with a low chuckle in his throat.

She brushed out of his gentle hold with a sly grin and finished fixing his plate, then gave it to him. "Then, maybe I should invite my husband to see what he's been missing for the last few weeks—since an invitation is the key?"

"Maybe." Lem put a finger into the potatoes and then into his mouth, slowly pulling his finger out as he walked.

"You still going to make one more tow tonight, or can one of the other guys maybe help Kenny?" His wife's question had come out on an impatient rush of air that turned her voice husky. "Or you gonna take a shower?"

"Yeah . . ."

"Yeah, what? A shower?"

"No."

"You're not making sense."

"You ain't making it easy to make sense."

"You still going?"

"Yeah, I'm going make a run for Kenny, but I'll be back."

"You won't be too tired later, will you?" Her voice was now a murmur and her smile had widened.

"No. Not with an invitation like that."

"I'ma hold you to it," she whispered. "I miss you, baby."

"I miss you, too." It was getting difficult to remember what he had to do for his brother-in-law, but he had to get out of there. "Look," he said, laughing. You need to feed my son and stop misbehavin'."

His wife laughed. "Oh, all right, party-pooper."

"We couldn't do anything anyway, until Jay eats and goes down for the night. I won't be in long after that."

He didn't trust himself to look at Bird as he shoveled forkfuls of mashed potatoes, string beans, and baked chicken into his mouth. He tried not to make a face. His wife was fine, but good Lord, some nights she just couldn't cook. The dry chicken almost made him choke, but he chewed extra hard to get it down with a smile. Jay had the right idea. The boy was using the food to do construction on his high-chair tray.

"You sure?" she said in a provocative tone with a wink.

"Bird, cut it out. I'm trying to eat. Can't a man eat his dinner in peace?"

She laughed. He tried to ignore her, but then had to laugh with her as she made a funny face at him and stuck out her tongue.

"Feed Jay, girl. Look at him. He's got more on his face than in his mouth."

"Don't tell me what I need to do, boy." She issued a knowing smile as she brushed past him.

He watched her saunter away to begin putting some of the food up. Finally. Thank God. He had to be on-point and stay focused. Everything he'd put on paper was going to be converted into a Power Point presentation for him, so he had to get the information down, then practice next week in front of the class, with the final goal to do his overview at the graduation ceremony. The pressure was on. He couldn't blame Bird for not understanding—how could she, when he hadn't told her everything yet?

Lem put a few more forkfuls into his mouth as he considered his dilemma. Sooner or later, he was going to have to break it to Bird that he was attempting to start his own business. Hopefully she'd understand that doing so had seeped into his veins like a virus, ever since he realized how well he could manage a business when the Joseph family had given him control of J&H Grocery. Hell, he'd turned the entire operation around on his own, and had made the family fat-bank, before the store burned down. Even Kenny knew he was *da man* when it came to business—because he'd helped Kenny get his thing organized over at Chadway Towing. Yeah, he was good at stuff like that. But he needed the Center in order to learn how to do a proposal and how to speak the language of banks. Having Bird strut around the kitchen, giving him sexy views of her perfect butt, messed up his focus.

Lem sighed, taking in more food. He was not going to lose focus. Not after working so hard to make his dream come to life. Those folks at the Center believed in him, and they weren't even family.

"I gotta go, baby," he said suddenly, standing and scooping a few more forkfuls into his mouth, then kissing her and Jay quickly. "Don't wanna be late for Kenny."

"Just half-eat my dinner and run off like the house is burning down, why don't you? I even made dessert."

"I'll eat it later."

He smiled at Bird as he passed her, ignoring the fact that her hands were now on her hips. She'd forgive all and understand all when she saw her man in front of a class of ten people with their families, wearing a suit, giving a Power Point slide overview like an executive, and doing a multimedia presentation complete with architectural blueprint renderings. He tugged on his jacket and whipped on his cap. She'd be happy after she saw him spout off financial projections as though he were a Harvard graduate, becoming a man who would make even her attorney sister, Teri, sit up and take note.

Oh yeah, his wife would be beyond thrilled when she saw that he was handling his business, that he would be able to move her and Jay into a classy home of their own one day soon, because his Bird could choose to work or not. But if she did, Bird would have the slammin' salon *of life*. And none of it would be a handout from anyone in the Joseph clan. He'd be his own man, would have a chance to finally prove that his past was the past, and that a brother from the projects could make it. All of it would be from honest sources, his own sweat-equity, through his investment in learning in class, as well as from his new coaches and support system he'd found one day, alone, on a tow run to the Community Development Corporation Center.

"Bye, baby," he yelled over his shoulder, and was out of the door.

Lem stood on the northwest corner of Forty-third and Calumet streets staring up at the old, abandoned Forum Building. Lucky breaks were hard to come by for a brother. Prison and the fast lane had taught him that much. But being in the joint was a long time ago, for crap he would never do again in life. People had to see that. He hoped they did.

This might be his ticket out of living on the edge. His final shot at escaping the border zone between the haves and have-nots. He wanted this opportunity so badly he could taste it.

His mind worked at his plan while his fingers constantly manipulated his tow truck keys over and over as though they were worry beads. The once-grand structure before him stood two stories high with a pitched roof, high arched windows, and was constructed of red brick. It was as though the exterior had now become the building's sexy red dress, and the curved windows were her sassy, arched eyebrows, putting a face on the entity that had consumed his attention like a lover. God had to hear his prayer.

His building, already firmly implanted in his mind as a living thing, was close to the El and other public transportation. She was magnificent for his plans, his dream. She was also in a part of historic Bronzeville that was slowly but quietly gentrifying—gated on one side by the housing projects on State Street, and by luxury apartments that could call an asking price of two-hundred thousand on the other. Beautiful.

Lem allowed his gaze to rove up and down the street, and then settle back upon the building. There was enough foot traffic in the area from the struggling Forty-third Street stores, and a diverse enough income level in the dense population to support her.

The best blues spot in town, the Checkerboard Lounge, was only two blocks east, and five blocks up on Forty-seventh, there were revitalization plans to turn that strip into a Blues District. He loved thinking about the new terms he'd learned in class, and was fixated on keeping that new vocabulary in his mind. He had to, lest he forget to use the right words in his final presentation.

His building was perfect. She was located right in the middle of Empowerment and Enterprise Zones, which meant that she offered crazy tax incentives with all sorts of access to other small-business support infrastructures, just because of where she sat. He loved the words that she required to describe her. Empowerment Zones, Enterprise Zones, infrastructure . . . yeah.

He closed his eyes, envisioning what the building could become. All she needed was somebody to treat her right. Just a little pampering, somebody to get his hands on her, who could appreciate her, and she'd shine again like a star.

Lem took in a slow, deep breath, trying to quell the excitement that was coursing through him, and opened his eyes. On the first floor she could host a first-rate restaurant, an Afrocentric bookstore and small café, possibly a full-blown health food store complete with fresh produce, and most important, a boutique and a day spa for his wife, Bird, to open. She'd always dreamed of expanding with a Cut It Up II.

It would be easy to make the argument that he and she could oversee the management of those operations. He had a solid background from the grocery store to lean on as demonstration of his ability to handle shops with multiple products—shoot, the grocery store had over a thousand items in it, with fresh produce, so why not? He'd have tenants and manage the building as though each store were a profit center. And Bird's success with her salon would be viewed positively, as well. Of course his baby could expand and run a day-spa. Bird was all that, when it came to business. They both were.

Lem began a slow stroll around the building. There was a spacious basement that would allow for a technology-literacy after-school program. Had to have that, not just for the money, but also to make good on his personal philosophy. The politics were a secondary issue. He tilted his head to peer up at his dream building.

If there had been an after-school program for him, who knows where he would have been by now? That was the one thing he'd always vowed—if he ever got a chance to do something big, he'd give something back. The politics were just another challenge to hurdle. The Center staff had told him that the after-school portion of the project would keep all community groups at bay, and get them on his side—strategic alliances. He could dig it. That always factored in, especially if folks were nervous.

He'd be sure to make it attractive, learning-focused, and he'd fill it with computers for neighborhood kids. The second floor could be renovated to house a spoken-word poetry and comedy club. Culture, education, economic development and positive entertainment would go over nice with all parties concerned, and stop any potential zoning bullshit. But it still got on his nerves that he had to play all these games with the system. What was the point to that madness?

Lem began walking again. Synergy... another new word he'd learned from his instructors. The sum of the whole was greater than the parts. He'd definitely drop that on 'em—*bam!* Everything in her would come together and fit like a glove. His creation would be about art, education, beauty, refinement, and would offer so much to his community and his family. That was real. He stopped once more and stared up. Yeah, this could work.

His strides had taken him around the entire perimeter of the structure while his mind ticked off the business points and figured revenues in his head. Blasts of wind and cold air charged at him, making his eyes water.

The rents from the shops would more than cover the mortgage. The after-school program rent would offer working capital to cover building upkeep and maintenance. The door cover charges, plus food and beverage sales from the second floor space would be solid, lucrative income. And all of it would create jobs for people living in the economically embattled area. All of it would be building something positive, something lasting—something that was finally *his*. But that would require a sudden miracle.

Maybe the instructors at the Community Development Corporation Center had a line on scoring a miracle—he sure as hell didn't. His record would reduce his chances of getting financing—despite the money he and Bird had saved up from his working, from the salon, and the settlement from the car accident she'd been in. Knowing his wife, she'd want to use it all to buy a house. She had to see that the better investment of that knot would be to put it into something that could grow faster than equity in a home. But Bird was stubborn.

Reality began to dampen his enthusiasm, and he slowly walked against the fall wind to climb back into his truck. The babble of radio dispatch calls jarred his senses. He put the vehicle in gear and pulled away from the curb, not even taking in the scenery as he drove down several streets and finally turned onto Martin Luther King Drive.

Where was an ex-con going to get nearly two hundred and fifty thousand dollars to do the renovations? Moreover, why on earth would the owners of this building take back the mortgage for a person with a past? After it was all said and done, even with the salon as collateral—*if* Bird would agree to go for that—along with their life savings, and even with his ability to prove that they both could manage the operation, his record would still stick out like a sore thumb.

Lem let out a low curse as he watched an empty potato chip bag catch in the wind and blow past the wheels of his truck down the street. "Damn!" Under any other circumstances, he and Bird would be the perfect candidates to get financing for a project like this. They had a successful enterprise, a third stake in a paid-off family residence, and cash in the bank.

On paper, they'd be viewed as Mr. and Mrs. Van Adams, a working-class, middle-income couple, with a bright future ahead of them—but with his record in the equation, their paper would be as good as the empty bag of chips that had blown by. His instructors at the Center were tripping. This was bullshit, and he'd been wasting his time on dreams.

"Yeah, that's me. I got it." Lem spoke sullenly into the tow truck radio microphone, reconfirming his agreement to pick up another tow.

Streets and traffic continued to pass by him in a blur as he made his way to the distressed vehicle. Seen one, you'd seen 'em all. But he loved being outside, in the streets, watching how easily you could turn one corner in Bronzeville and find upscale town houses or luxury apartments, and then suddenly be near the projects or in the badlands if you went the wrong way.

What had he been thinking when he'd lied to his wife, and told her he was volunteering at a community center every Wednesday night? She hadn't believed him at first, and rightfully so. His whole set of arguments for doing this so-called volunteer work sounded bogus to his own ears when he'd said it. No wonder Bird had called over there, but his game was smooth.

He was lucky that once his wife got through to the evening secretary, and spoke to an instructor who'd told her he was in class, she'd relaxed. But he'd still wasted nearly twelve weeks on this secret entrepreneurial project—to what end? A surprise for her and the family that might not pan out in the long run . . . might just be a stupid dream.

His instructors didn't know what it was like to be a black man with a past. Putting his thoughts on paper, carefully categorizing them into a marketing section, an operations section, and a financial projections section for a business plan, was theoretical garbage. In the end, a man needed money to convert a dream into reality.

Lem let his breath out hard, hopped out of his truck, and dealt with the stalled car on the side of the road.

Bringing his vehicle to a stop after his last tow, Lem sat in the truck and stared at the sign above the entrance door to his job. Chadway Towing. "God bless the child who's got his own," he muttered.

His brother-in-law, Kenny, had his own thing going on, and could put his wife, Maxine, and their children into their own home. Any man wanted to be able to do that. Kenny was his own boss, his own man, and was even cool enough to share some crumbs from the Chadway table by giving him a job. Lem didn't begrudge what his brother-in-law had accomplished, but why not him, too? Kenny was a workhorse, had made his business from his hands. You had to respect that. The whole family did. But why was it so ridiculous for *him* to get some basic respect—when his mind was sharp, and his work ethic now solid? As much as he appreciated the help from

Kenny, he needed more. He needed something to call *his* own.

Lem shook the uncomfortable feeling and opened the vehicle door. Kenny was his boy. Wasn't Kenny's fault that things went the way they did. Luck of the draw, Lem reminded himself. Luck of the goddamned draw. Fate had given him the lot of being born to parents who didn't handle their business and had raised him in a crazy environment; Kenny simply wasn't dealt that hand. That made all the difference in the world. The way a brother started out had a lot to do with options and the way he finished up—which was why he was gonna do this thing. He'd handle his business. Jay was *not* going to be left up to the luck of the draw or a hand dealt by the streets. He wasn't putting Bird through that, either—watching her son get pulled into the street life with tears in her eyes and a heavy heart.

A slight pang of guilt for momentarily feeling the way he did about Kenny accosted Lem as he slammed the truck door and loped toward the dispatch office. Kenny had given him a chance, had his back and, as a friend and family member, he owed Kenny support in his new city towing contract.

Maybe it was the fact that he owed everybody so much that wore on him. If he thought about it real hard, he owed crazy debts of gratitude to all of them.

He owed his wife, Bird, for waiting for him while he was away and for putting up with all his employment drama when he got out. He owed the Joseph sisters, for allowing him and Bird and Jay to live in their parents' house until they could get straight. Even though Bird owned a third of it, her sisters *could* have voted to sell it. So what that Bird wanted to live there, and her sisters agreed—he didn't want to live in her dead parents' home, as much as he'd loved Momma Joe. He wanted his own place, one that he could afford for them to buy, where he wouldn't have to call a family meeting if he wanted to change the paint color on the freakin' walls. Why couldn't Bird see that?

It was cold as hell outside. Lem boxed his arms to warm up as he strode across the lot. Large puffs of steam came out of his mouth in the frigid early-evening air. His brother-in-law owned everything he surveyed as he passed rows of parked tow trucks. The name Chadway was on everything. One day . . .

Lem hailed a couple of the guys who were standing outside catching a smoke.

"Yo!" Lem called toward them, receiving a series of return "yo" acknowledgments from each of them.

The cold air felt like a blade on his face. Managing the grocery store was way better than this . . . too bad it had burned down. Bullshit luck. Thinking about that only reminded him that he even owed Hardy Lester, for allowing him a chance to prove that he could manage money and be honorable, by giving Lem power of attorney to run his half of J&H Grocery. It was like one thing led to another with that, doubling his debt to the rest of the Joseph family, especially Kenny, for having his back, and believing that he was honest and could do it. He owed them for trusting him. Go figure. It had practically taken an act of Congress to get everybody to agree to merely let him ring the register in that store at first. But being an entrepreneur was now seriously in his blood, and what's more, he'd proven to them all that he could do it.

Lem stood outside the main door for a moment. He needed to gather his thoughts before he faced Kenny. Bitterness ripped through his memories as he thought about how he'd owed Teri for financing his and Bird's wedding, for giving Bird a loan to open her salon, and for helping him to beat a bad rap when all fingers pointed to him as the one who might have torched the family store. It was like being in the joint without bars, always having to tell somebody about every stinking move he made, or decision he wanted to make.

"Hey, man," one of his coworkers called out. "Cold as a witch's titty today!"

"Ain't snowing and icing up yet, though," Lem yelled back.

"That's when we get paid, bro. Don't talk bad about Mother Nature."

Lem nodded. Yeah. He couldn't control the weather or his destiny. Everyone but him seemed to control his destiny. He felt like he was *still* serving time, obliged by more than honor to help Kenny get on his feet with the heavy new contract he had been awarded by the city, because it could set up Chadway Towing, as well as Kenny's household, for life.

For Better, For Worse   41

Lem's thoughts struggled within him, but it was too cold to hang outside. He opened the outer door and immediately went to the kerosene heater Kenny kept by the door for the men. He wondered if there would ever be a way to make his wife and his best friend understand that, while he appreciated everything they'd done for him, there were some things a man just needed to do for himself.

"Yo, man, how's it hangin'?" Kenny asked.

"Cool," Lem replied as the inner door slammed behind him. "Same ol', same ol.' "

"It was a rough one, I take it?" Kenny asked more slowly, glancing at Lem for a moment, and then taking a telephone call.

Lem didn't answer as his brother-in-law handled the call, but simply waited for Kenny to hang up the receiver as he dropped into a chair facing the desk.

"Got anything else for me before I punch out?"

Kenny stared at Lem before responding.

"You cool, man? Everything all right at home?"

"Yeah. Just beat. Wind is cuttin' like a razor. You know the deal."

"Well, second shift is on, so you can punch out unless you need some OT tonight."

"I always need some overtime," Lem muttered. "Thanks, but tonight I promised Bird I'd get home at a decent time. She's been edgy since I started volunteering—it keeps me out late. You know the deal."

"Well, if it's stressing you to this degree, bro, why don't you give it up and—"

"Because I gave them my word I would do the full

twelve weeks," Lem snapped, standing quickly, and pacing toward the door. "I just came in to see if you were good with the second shift and it would be cool for me to call it a night."

"Chill. I'm cool in here," Kenny said, his voice holding a tone of concern. "All I was saying is that you look like you need some rest, but you do what you gotta do. We're all right, I'm good."

Lem nodded, trying to force the aggravation out of his next response. "I'm just a little edgy from the long day, bro, and this commitment was more than I bargained for. I'm gonna give it up after this class graduates. Was just a little somethin' I thought I should do . . . you know, give back to the community and all. But I've gotta be realistic. Stop pipe dreamin' about helping other people and whatnot. Need to get my damned self straight first, before I start some new shit."

"I can dig it," Kenny agreed as he stood and walked toward Lem. "How many more weeks you got?"

Lem could feel his secret bubbling up inside his chest, trying to come up his throat and past his lips. But he swallowed it away. For once, he wanted to have something complete to show them. Just once, he wanted to be able to come to them with everything tied up in a neat package that they didn't have to fix, advise him about, or intervene to make right. So, he'd hold the surprise until it was ready, and then he would be able to accept the cheers of congratulations for doing something all by himself—his way.

For Better, For Worse

"Today I had to run by there for a minute, and then two more Wednesday nights."

Kenny extended his fist and Lem pounded it. The phone rang again.

"Brother, you can hang for two more Wednesdays," his brother-in-law chuckled as he picked up the receiver. "Piece of cake."

three

"I don't need this nonsense, Teri," Bird said into the phone. "That class is supposed to run from seven to nine on Wednesday nights, and it only takes a half hour to get home. Now he says that he went earlier in the day, but had to make another tow run for Kenny—which is why he isn't home now, when he should be—since there was no class tonight. Here it is almost eleven o'clock, in the middle of the week, and his ass is still out in the streets."

Bird held the telephone receiver hard against her face in the dark, keeping the covers on the bed up over her shoulders to block the night chill.

"Bird, we've been over this a hundred times in the past, and you know how I feel about your husband. But if I say something wrong about Lem, then eventually I'm the bad guy. No matter what happens, you two always kiss and make up, and then I'm the mean, wicked sister who didn't trust your man. So all I can say is, if you have concerns regarding his whereabouts, *again*, then you should confront him and stick to your guns."

Why was her sister trying to be logical at a time when it was all about how she felt, not what was intellectually correct. Bird let out a long sigh. "That's just it, Teri. I'm tired of always confronting Lem about something."

"What do you want from this relationship, then?"

Her sister's question hung in the air as a long pause in the conversation came between them.

"I just want him to be honest, I suppose, and to do right without me having to stay on top of him."

Again, there was a pause. She could tell that Teri was grappling with a response, and appreciated that her sister didn't just come back with a fast, attorney-type retort.

"Maybe he is being honest with you, Bird," her sister finally said in a gentle tone.

"I don't understand."

"His actions have been consistent, honey. Ever since the day you two hooked up. Right?"

"Well . . ."

"Think about it," Teri argued in a soft voice. "He has always been a street rogue. He has tried to conform to family-man standards for you, but somehow Lem always winds up back in the streets, or involved in some mess. When he first came home from prison for dealing drugs, he said he couldn't find a job—and went back to running the streets, and you guys separated but eventually got back together. Then—"

"Okay, okay," Bird cut in. "I know all that. But he promised that—"

"Ask yourself, how many of these same promises

have been broken? Ask yourself, what about him are you looking for that is just not there?" Teri took a breath and let it out hard. "Ask yourself, can you be at peace with knowing who he really is, and can you and Jay deal with that? Because to do any less is living in denial. People, by and large, I have found, do not fundamentally change. They may attempt to change, they may tone down some behaviors, but people follow the path that they know best."

"He's a good father, Teri."

Strain crackled in the silence between the sisters for a moment before Teri's voice interjected.

"You're changing the subject. He has never been a so-called bad father, Bird. That has been consistent. But he has never truly been the husband you've wanted, either."

Bird sat up in bed, shaking her head. "Not true, Teri. Lem has a very loving, tender side that other people don't see."

"Define good husband for me, Bird," Teri immediately shot back. "You have defined a good boyfriend, maybe a good lover. But what does it take to be a good husband?"

Bird found her voice slowly. How could she argue with a sister who was a skilled debater, especially about something she hadn't figured out all the way herself yet?

"I don't know," Bird whispered. "Maybe somebody who comes home every night, who takes care of his family, is a good provider . . . who is like a good friend."

"Is Lem any of these things?"

"Yeah, in a way . . ."

"All right," Teri snapped.

"Why do you always have to do that?"

"Do what?" Teri fussed. "Get sick and tired of you making excuses for him?"

"I don't make excuses for my husband, Teri. I don't have to!"

"Oh, then forgive me because I am worried about my sister's welfare and state of mind. Excuse me for not fully hearing that this is a man who comes home consistently every night and that his wife knows, without a reasonable doubt, his whereabouts. My apology, Bird."

Teri's words felt like a harsh reality slap. Bird didn't want to talk to her sister any longer; this was not why she'd called her.

"Look, I gotta go. We're fine. I was just . . . forget it. I'll talk to you later."

"You always do this, Bird. Makes me crazy."

"Do what, Teri? Try to stick up for Lem before you convict him without a judge or jury?"

"No. Always call me or Maxine with a problem, and then when we tell you what you don't want to hear, you have to get off the telephone."

Bird could feel her grip tighten on the telephone. She loved her sister, but she could be such a bitch. "Make your point, Teri."

"Number one," Teri said, obviously not caring that Bird was totally peeved, "you have told me that since this man's newfound volunteerism began—something way outside his character structure—he has not been making love to you with any regularity or fervor. Am I wrong, Bird? Stop me if I'm incorrect in my assumptions."

Now Teri was not fighting fair—she didn't have to go there. Bird swallowed hard as tears formed in her eyes and threatened to fall. She should never have told her sister about that. She hated when Teri went legal on her, putting her on the witness stand—no matter how right her sister might be. Even though she understood that her sister was trying hard to fill the shoes of their lost family matriarch, and that Teri's hard-line approach to things came from a good place in her heart, sometimes it was too much to cope with.

Bird felt a sigh push its way up her throat. She loved her sister; she loved her husband. Lem was a never-ending argument between them, and they'd visited these issues a hundred times before. Teri didn't like Lem, so there was no reasoning with her about him. Bird loved Lem, but also knew his flaws. She couldn't really get mad at Teri, because a lot of what her sister said was true. On the other hand, Teri just didn't understand. Putting up a fight in Lem's defense would only prolong the conversation that she now wanted to end. Maybe she should have called Maxine.

"No rebuttal? Okay, then let's go on to point number two: Lem being a good provider. That's never happened on a consistent basis. He has just started making a good salary since the store closed, and now with Chadway—"

"The man has banked ten grand from hard work, Sis. Back off that one. He's now a good—"

"But, before, you were always the one bailing him out, literally and figuratively."

"That was *before*, and doesn't matter now. He brings home the bacon, Teri. He makes as much with the overtime as I do at the salon."

She'd gone to bed worried about whether her husband actually went where he said he was going, and angry about Lem choosing to volunteer over spending some time with her, but now she was ready to fight for him. Wasn't nobody coming between her and her man, not even a well-meaning but off-the-wall sister. Not even her favorite sister. Shit. She'd just rock her man's world when he got in, fix whatever was wrong between them, and go about their business. Teri had better get out of their business.

"I can see that this conversation is going nowhere, Bird," Teri said in a huff. "All I know is, you are the consistent financial backbone of the family. Sure, he does his best when employed, but what if his situation changes again? And why is he always in an uncertain financial position?"

Bird opened her mouth to provide an answer, but Teri's legal swiftness cut Bird off.

"Because he never committed himself to be disciplined enough to get some education, to hold permanent employment somewhere once he found it, and to take the burden off of you so that you can even consider having another child, Bird."

"Not true, and you know it. He ran J&H like a

champ, and he's Kenny's backbone at the tow company. Get off it, Teri. Let the past rest."

"And being a friend . . . Oh, God, you don't want me to get started on that subject of honesty and integrity." Relentless, Teri had switched gears in a deft tactical move.

"He is a good friend, Teri," Bird found herself whispering through her teeth. "It was hard for him to find a job after being away, you know that."

"Do you hear yourself, Bird?"

"He . . . he . . . well, he took care of me after the car accident. He was right there, Teri. That has to count for something."

"True. And a good friend doesn't make his wife feel unattractive by staying away from her intimately just because her physical condition temporarily, or permanently, changed. He hurt your self-esteem with that bull. If he was such a good friend, then why did you have to resort to threatening to go to strip in a strip joint to get his attention? Remember that? And why in the hell would he take Kenny, of all people, to a strip joint? Maxine still has that stuck in her craw, even though they've patched up that little debacle. Answer me that, Bird."

Silence sliced through Bird's spirit, stabbing her in the most tender portion of it. She did not want to ever mentally revisit how ashamed she'd been when she couldn't hold her bladder after being injured in the car accident, nor did she ever want to look back on what wearing adult diapers did to her sense of femininity or independence. Worse yet, was how much she just wanted to curl up in a fetal position and die when her husband admitted the truth: the diapers turned him off. She'd wanted to forgive and forget and never look back at that dark time in her marriage. It had lasted only for a short period, and was over; she was healed now. That was almost a year ago. But maybe Teri was right. Maybe she didn't want to know the stark truth.

Tears of frustration and anger and hurt fell. She was no longer able to keep them behind the guardrail of tough talk or stubborn will. Damn, Teri knew how to push her buttons—always did. Slowly easing herself beneath the covers, Bird curled up into a little ball, cradling the phone against her cheek as she silently wept. Her husband had issues, that was true. But she still loved him. One day they'd do something together, without anybody's help, and show them all. They would stand united. They'd show them! Just because they were the youngest didn't mean they always had to take everybody's advice.

"Bird . . . Bird . . . Honey, I'm sorry," Teri softly called into the receiver. "Don't cry, sweetie. I know you love him. I'm sorry, Bird."

Although she'd heard what her sister had said, no words could form in Bird's mouth. Only a rush of the feelings she'd thought had been released and washed away came flooding back to envelop her.

"Baby . . . oh . . . come on, Bird. You know you're pretty, and sexy, and fun, and smart, and beautiful," her sister lamented through the telephone. "This is why I get so angry at him."

Still Bird could not speak, only a soft whimper

came out. It wasn't always Lem who did things to her, or hurt her with words. Teri had no idea how much the words hurt, coming from the sister Bird most admired for her accomplishments. Nor would Teri ever be able to understand just how important her opinion of Lem really was. Bird had called Teri for approval, for confidence that Lem's volunteering was a good thing. She'd wanted one of Teri's logical statements to fill her ear about how volunteering in the community helped his résumé, and showed that he was making strides. She wanted Teri to see the progress he was making, and chastise her for being silly to worry when the man was doing right. She had not called her sister for this ration of bullshit. Both sisters stayed on the line without saying anything for what seemed like a long time.

"I just want him to love me, and be there for me and Jay. . . . I want to feel like we're a priority, and that he still finds me attractive, and that we're each other's best friend. Is that too much to ask?"

Teri's voice was slow in answering. "Isn't that what any of us wants from a man? I've made some choices I've had to live with, too. I have two ex-husbands and some serious relationships gone awry to show for it, and loved them anyway. Guess I'm not a complete expert on the subject, sweetie. So, I can't be too hard on you, can I?"

Her sister's question held her, and the melancholy in Teri's tone made Bird wipe her face and unfurl from the balled-up position she'd been in.

"I guess we've both been through it with these men,

huh?" Bird chuckled and sniffed, and was pleasantly surprised when Teri joined her.

"Yeah," Teri said with a sad chuckle followed by a sniff. "It's hard to get this personal relationship stuff right. I just want the best for you, and overdid it with the protective big sister thing. Sorry."

"I hear you, and apology accepted," Bird replied, wiping her face with her palm. "If you love them, then you're gonna go through changes with them, I suppose." *This* was the sister she wanted to talk to, the side of Teri she'd needed to connect with—that soft, loving side that nobody in the family but her seemed to be able to reach or see.

"Yes, but all I'm asking that you do is to find your personal limits. Define what you will and will not put up with, and then the rest is negotiable. But you have to draw a line in the sand with regard to some issues."

"Yup." Much revived, Bird pushed herself back up to a sitting position. Talking to Teri, in some ways, was just like talking to her mother . . . and the dearly missed communion soothed her. "Like I'm not having drugs in my home or in our lives."

"Good."

"And I'm not dealing with him cheating."

"Excellent."

"I want honesty, and to know where he is."

"That's critical for trust."

"And I deserve to be made to feel like I'm special."

"Absolutely."

"If he does those things," Bird said with confidence, "then together we can work on the financial aspects—as long as he's trying to do the right thing. He does have some hurdles, because he made really stupid decisions in the past. I knew that going in, and it won't change overnight."

"Okay," Teri agreed, but with a slight hesitation that implied there was a "but" coming. "That's being realistic. You know what resources the man is dealing with, so you have realistic expectations. That's smart . . . healthy."

"Right."

"However—"

Bird laughed, cutting off her sister's rebuttal at the pass. "I knew there was a *but.*"

Teri laughed, a genuine chuckle laced with affection. "Buuuut," she said sheepishly, "he cannot lean on that issue as a crutch forever. He needs to make some serious plans to work his way out of that situation. That's what you all should be discussing, and what he should be devoting any shred of extra time toward: creating a platform for advancement to make up for the lost time, the lost opportunities, and the lost financial security that he, by his own hand, created."

"That's why he's out at night volunteering and giving something back to the community he took from," Bird retorted.

They both laughed easily.

"Touché. But, you should not have to suffer for the rest of your life because your man made some wrong choices in the past." Teri's voice had lost its once strident quality. Firm tenderness replaced her argumentative tone, just like her mother's voice would have.

"Nor should my nephew, Jay," Teri added with a sigh. "I won't have my baby sister and my darling nephew conscripted into a life at the edge of opportunity, always having your noses pressed up against the glass, because Lem is whining about the system, what chances he didn't have, and so on and on and on. He needs to get over it and get on with it, and to do something with his life."

This time her sister's words didn't make Bird want to crumble. Oddly, they gave her renewed strength.

"That's right, Teri. Everything Lem has told me before—all the excuses, everything had to do with his terrible childhood, then how he got busted because he didn't have the right role models, then how getting busted followed and haunted him, and then how much drama it was to get employed—has to stop. It's like a never-ending story."

"Well, God bless you, Bird," Teri said with triumph. "Now we're getting somewhere!"

"Okay. So, he's a good father," Bird responded quickly, ticking off in her mind the character traits of her husband as she spoke. "That's positive. He doesn't cheat, doesn't hit me or call me out of my name."

"Bird, *that's basic*. He doesn't get brownie points for that. If he did abuse you, we'd find a way to get him locked up, or find some of Daddy's old gambling friends on the wrong side of the tracks to just kill the man. Okay?"

"All right, all right. I hear you," Bird added with a

chuckle. "Point well taken. And, we do, *normally*, have a good physical relationship."

"Bird, that's not—"

"Teri," Bird interrupted. "You said be real and know what you need. I need *that* in my life. It is a serious part of what I want to have in my marriage, okay?"

"All right, I concede. Continue."

"Thank you."

Laughter came through the receiver.

"All right, where was I?" Bird fussed with good nature.

"The part about how you needed to get some, in order to function," Teri teased, making them both giggle.

"Right. For real, for real."

"You all also need to talk honestly," Teri added. "You said you wanted him to be your friend."

"He is, in a lot of ways." Bird's voice had become soft as she remembered quiet talks, how Lem would bathe her when she had a hard day, and how he cared for her after the car accident. She could envision his face, the love in his eyes, the worry and concern, and how gently he'd cradle her in his arms. Nothing in the world could describe that sense of safety and comfort. There was a tender side to him that was hers alone to see.

How could one put into words what it meant to have someone love you and accept your family, to be there as your parents passed away? She thought of the small kindnesses they'd exchanged as lovers, friends, and as man and wife. For better, for worse, for richer or for poorer, in sickness and in health . . . There was no way to quantify their intimate pillow talk, or the peace that enveloped her soul when they'd lie together on the sofa, the baby on Lem's chest, simply doing nothing, just being.

"You still there?"

Teri's question brought her out of her reverie with a jolt.

"Yes. Thanks, Sis, for talking to me. I know he just probably stopped on the way home to have a beer, or something. Lem is a good man, and I suppose I miss him, is all." She was so glad she'd talked to Teri, and had gotten all of the drama out of her system before her husband came home.

"You know to call me if it's anything different than that, right?"

Bird heard a vehicle coming down the street, and a wave of excitement surged through her. "I think I hear him coming home now, so I'd better go."

"Well, I'm glad that I could help while away the time with your horny, evil butt, and go through your personal catharsis until he came home."

"I love you, too, Sis. Thanks."

"Bye, baby," Teri said gently. "Get off the phone and go get you some."

Bird blotted her face with a tissue from the nightstand as she hung up the telephone, then quietly slipped back down under the covers. She felt so much better, and he'd kept his word. *He was home.* Where his rusty butt should be.

The front door opened, and she could hear Lem going through his routine. His footsteps stopped at the foyer entrance, and she knew he was hanging his jacket on a hook and taking off his cap. More footsteps went toward the kitchen. She smiled. No matter what the hour, he always went to the kitchen first, opened the fridge, and stood there with the door open for a while—deciding. The man was an eating machine, always hungry. Bird closed her eyes and a sense of peace claimed her without dulling the growing anticipation that created little butterflies in her belly. Maybe this was what she craved: the pure knowing. It was the same peace she'd seen on her mother's face.

The sound of heavy boots coming up the stairs made it hard for Bird to keep her eyes closed, but she wanted to appear that she'd been asleep. Having Lem think she'd waited up or didn't trust him would blow the groove, and tonight she so badly needed there to be a groove. All she could do was pray that he'd had a positive evening, that nothing had spoiled his mood.

The sound of the shower going on made her heartbeat quicken. If he was too tired, he would have just dragged himself into the room, dropped his work duds where he'd stood, and then fallen into bed. *But he was in the shower.*

"Victoria's Secret, don't fail me," she whispered and quietly giggled, adjusting the strap on her dark purple silk teddy, and taking a sexy, feigned sleeping pose in the bed.

Carefully pulling back the covers to give her husband a glimpse of what she was wearing, Bird tried to

For Better, For Worse

steady her breathing. She reveled in the fact that her husband still had this effect on her—after all these years, all their drama, and even a baby, this man whom she loved made her feel this way.

When she heard the bathroom door open, her stomach did a tiny flip-flop. Pretending to be asleep was becoming increasingly difficult as renewed anticipation swept through her. She forced herself to keep her eyes closed, and then gave in to simply keeping her lids lowered to slits so that she could see him when he came into the room. She knew that in the dark, he wouldn't be able to tell that she was spying on him. She also knew it was silly, but she loved the game.

Her talk with her sister had helped her remember why she loved him. Arguing with Teri did that—it made her mind close ranks against an outside-of-her-marriage invader to protect the relationship within it. His footsteps down the hall nearly made her hold her breath, and when he slipped into the bedroom wearing only a towel, she couldn't play her game any longer.

Moonlight and luminescence from the streetlamps outside the bedroom window glistened against his moist, dark skin as he stood at the foot of their bed. Her gaze traveled up his six-foot frame, lingering over her man's tight, muscular abdomen, which was defined by six bricks that converted into two large cinder blocks at his chest. His jawline was covered in a neatly trimmed beard, and her line of vision found his full lips, rimmed by a thin mustache, before it settled upon the full beauty of his handsome face. God, she loved his mouth. The thought of what those full lips could do to her . . .

"You waited up," he murmured.

"Yeah, I did," she replied in a breathy whisper. "You didn't eat all your dinner, and left before you had dessert."

"I told you I'd eat dessert later," he murmured, slowly pulling the towel away from his body.

Their eyes met, and he climbed onto the foot of the bed as though stalking her on all fours, without breaking their intense gaze. Just short of her feet, he stopped and gently pulled the covers away, leaving her exposed.

His cheek grazed the inside of her calf, as he gently spread her legs. A kiss landed upon her knee, and she closed her eyes as a trail of kisses found their way up her inner thigh. Witnessing his arousal, the way his eyes swept over her body, sent a tremor through her. This game was so much fun.

Her belly button was invaded by a fluttering lick that sent a spasm of pleasure through her. She closed her eyes again. God, what he was doing felt so good.

"What was for dessert?" he asked.

"Ice cream," she breathed out with a small giggle.

"Oh. But I thought you said you made dessert," he murmured against her belly, and then allowed his tongue to sweep across it in a broad, burning lick.

"I was going to make sundaes," she whispered, shivering from his attention. "I bought all the stuff for it."

"Really?" he asked low in his throat. "Then I stand corrected."

For Better, For Worse

Her answer was a breathy exhalation and her chin tilted up to give him her throat. His mouth immediately responded to her offering, his lips caressing her neck, her collarbone, down the center of her chest.

Why was her husband trying to drive her out of her mind? He was going to make her beg him in a minute, if he didn't stop playing.

Well, two could play at that game!

"Somebody is in a much-improved mood this morning," Kenny said on a yawn as he and Lem stood outside the garage.

"I'm cool." Lem shrugged, turning his head to hide the wide grin on his face.

"Bet your ass is tired," Kenny remarked with a sly wink while fumbling with the keys to open the outer office door. "But there's tired, then again, there's thank-your-Jesus-good-tired."

"I suppose so." Lem laughed as he remembered that he had actually called upon God while making love to Bird last night. "Yeah."

"Uh huh." Kenny chuckled as they entered the building and turned on the lights. "Wish I could be tired like that a little more often, brother."

"Right—you're the one with three kids 'cause you and Max can't keep your hands to yourselves."

The two fell into companionable laughter as Kenny slapped Lem's shoulder.

The best part of working with his brother-in-law was that they were friends. If only he could sit down with Kenny and tell him how much was going on.

Kenny had been there; he knew the anxieties of being an entrepreneur, and he could understand how much a man needed to have his own domain and destiny. Kenny had experience in this thing he was about to do. Moreover, Lem didn't want his venture to come between them, ruin the laughs, the sense of family, or the peace. It could all be so cool if everybody could just see it, understand and be happy for him and Bird. In truth, he didn't know what he'd do without the sense of connectedness to his family . . . this insane, irritating, but loving bunch of folks who very often got on his nerves.

"Yo, man, thanks," Lem said in a quiet voice, offering his fist for Kenny to pound.

"Thanks for what?" Kenny pounded Lem's fist, giving him a quizzical expression.

"For everything, man. For being my family, and always havin' my back."

"You know I always got your back. You're my family, and thanks for always having mine."

"Yeah, see, that's just the thing—"

"Look at you," Kenny cut in with a laugh. "Gettin' all sentimental first thing in the morning. I've been there." Kenny went to his desk, shaking his head. "Whoooo-weee! Girl musta turned your black behind inside out last night. You standing here smiling like a Cheshire cat one minute, then all of a sudden look like you about to bust into tears like you just got saved in church. Dang."

Kenny's infectious laughter made Lem smile, despite the fact that it no longer seemed like the right time to broach the subject. This was how he always wanted to see his best friend—successful, laughing about dumb shit, living life easy and to the max. Kenny was good people and deserved that.

"I gotta admit that it was sort of a religious experience, man. I ain't quite right yet from it." Lem chuckled.

"Well, let the church say, *Amen*," Kenny boomed as he shook his head. "And, while we're at it, please tell Maxine to pass the plate. Giving is divine, I'm told, and your sister-in-law ain't even tithing."

Lem could tell Kenny was just teasing him, making up stories to keep the conversation going so he could rib him. The corners of Kenny's eyes crinkled as he kept his focus on messing with him, then issued a wink. Was last night that obvious?

"That ain't my business, man," Lem said, laughing. "I'm out of it, and don't mess up my salvation by tellin' Bird I said anything to you about nuthin'."

Kenny sat down, took the keys from his desk, and turned them before his lips as though locking his mouth. "I won't say a mumblin' word."

"I'm serious," Lem warned in fun. "You don't know how long . . . I mean, seriously, man. Things gotta stay cool for a while in my house."

Kenny started making little jerky motions while clearing his desk, badly imitating a nervous twitch. "Oh, I know what's it's like to be strung out, brother," he said, teasing Lem. "I know . . . I . . . I . . . I mean, I know," he stammered, "what needin' a fix is all about . . . damn, your supply dries up and whatnot, and it's all jacked up, you're all messed up for a while till you can get straight. I won't blow your supply man, that is, unless you hook a brother up, see what I'm sayin'? Make Bird talk to Maxine about my rations."

All Lem could do was holler with laughter at his brother-in-law, who was cutting the fool. He couldn't stop chuckling as he thought of the look on Kenny's face if he ever *did* say something to Bird to tell Max—about anything, but especially *that*. Kenny would have a stroke if anybody got into his business. Please.

"It's too early in the morning for you to be on my case, Kenny. Now, give me my runs so I can get outta here. I ain't tellin' Bird jack to tell Maxine. My name is Bennett, and I ain't in it!"

But the game was in full swing, and there was no way to avoid it. He was cold-busted, and his brother-in-law wasn't having any mercy this morning.

"But see," Kenny pressed on. "Like, you got time, 'cause no calls have come in yet, and we ain't got the boot-and-tow list for today faxed to us yet. And Maxine, she's still mad at me over—"

"I told you, I ain't in it, man." Lem shook his head and tried to edge his way out the door in search of coffee. "You stay in trouble with that sweet woman. I ain't—"

"Ooops, see ya got in my business," Kenny joked. "How is it that I'm the one always in trouble? The pot is callin' the kettle black on that one."

"I don't know," Lem sighed, giving up the coffee

search and plopping down in the chair. "What happened this time?"

"You know she's trying to do this artistic thing now. Poetry. *Writing.*"

"Okay. But that's cool, right?"

"No, that's not necessarily cool," Kenny fussed in good nature, standing to go make a pot of coffee.

Deep. Lem shook his head. If his brother-in-law would stop tripping about the nonsense, there could be peace over at the Chadway household. Okay, now he knew the deal. There'd been a spat; Kenny wasn't looking for advice, as per usual, or somebody to get in it—just validation. Lem sighed. It didn't have to be all this. If only his own problems were so easy.

"What, may I ask, and only because you are *making* me ask, is so uncool about Maxine's poetry?"

Kenny stood before the coffeemaker as the grungy pot filled with near-black liquid that was supposed to be coffee.

"I'm not sure," Kenny finally said, all mirth slipping out of his voice. "It's like she's not happy just being home anymore. Ever since she had to work in here for me a little bit, she keeps looking for other things . . . even ran for public office. I love her and all, but between me and you, I was glad she lost—even though I was proud of her trying—'cause that would have been havoc around my house if she'd won. Now *she's writing.* I don't know."

The laughs that they had just shared had dissipated. It was like being outside on a sunny day, and then all of a sudden clouds pass over, leaving the street gray and the mood somber. If Kenny felt like that about his own wife, then what would he think about him, simply a brother-in-law, trying to expand his dreams and leave the fold of the predictable? Would Kenny be pissy, and then say he wanted him to do well, while all the while hoping that he'd fail? Lem wasn't sure, and he didn't like being unsure of where Kenny stood on things like this.

"Here's what I know," Lem finally said, his tone easy but firm. "Everybody gets tired of doing the same thing all the time—but that doesn't mean that you stop loving the people you're with."

Silence briefly enveloped the two, and Lem wondered if now would be the time to edge toward the subject he needed to broach with his friend.

"Take me, for example," he offered. "Yesterday, I was really sick and tired of picking up tows."

"Yeah, but that's natural," Kenny countered. "There are days when I don't feel like coming in here, or dealing with whatever hassle is facing me, too."

"And that's why there's a thing called a day off, or vacation, right?"

"Yeah," Kenny hedged. "I suppose."

"Well, being at home with the kids all the time doesn't allow for that day off or vacation, brother. I know when Bird is working all day at the salon, then on top of it, I'm late and Jay is giving her the blues, she ain't exactly in the mood to tolerate no bullshit from me when I walk in the door. And you got three of them, and—"

"But I—"

"Naw, hear me out, Kenny. Seriously. You got three over there, and Max don't even get a chance to just do something she likes every now and then—with other adults. Plus, she ain't as wild and crazy as Bird, and in that regard, you're lucky. When Bird gets bored, she does off-the-hook kinda shit that requires a full-family intervention. You ain't got that to contend with. Am I wrong?"

Kenny laughed with Lem and they pounded fists again, both men remembering the many times Bird went to extremes to prove a point.

"Maxine never sashayed out to a strip club and threatened to strip after we got busted going to one, did she? Cured me, though. Ain't been to one since."

Kenny shook his head, smiling, and then began to pour them both mugs of coffee. "You said it, I didn't, and I don't ever want you saying I said anything about Bird that will start some mess, because I didn't." He handed Lem a cup of coffee, and both men took a swig of their respective mugs at the same time and grimaced.

"You got to get a new coffeemaker in here, brother. I'm not playin'."

"You ain't told a lie, Lem. But I'm saving money."

"Kenny, you are the cheapest—"

"I'm just frugal," Kenny argued with a laugh. "You all can't appreciate how pennies can add up to dollars."

"Penny wise and pound foolish." Lem just shook his head.

"But you're changing the subject. What am I going

to do about Maxine and her newest, crazy brainstorm?"

"All right," Lem said, setting down the bitter brew on Kenny's desk, and resuming his argument where he'd left off. "If the sister is sitting at home, writing in a journal, or going to a class every now and again, what's the problem?"

"I guess you're right," Kenny admitted with a shrug.

"You know she loves your big Lurch ass to death, right?"

Kenny just chuckled.

"Might wanna ask her to read you some of her poems in bed." Lem gave him a wink.

"Aw, man, I ain't no sixteenth-century knight, tryin' to read some love sonnet when I'm tryin' to get—"

"Brother, brother, brother," Lem said in a quiet tone, pointing to his temple as he spoke. "If her head is right and tight," he offered with a chuckle, his pointed finger lowering slowly, "then . . ."

"My head will be right and tight."

"Simplistic. If class chills her out, or writing makes her cool, then flow with it."

"You think so, brother-in-law?"

Kenny's expression was so awestruck that Lem could only laugh and shake his head again.

"Hell, yeah," Lem said. "I might even take a class one day myself."

"Poetry? Get out of here!" Kenny walked away from him and began sorting the mail on his desk, picking through it for checks and bills.

"Naw. Business classes."

There. It had been said. It was out on the table. All Lem could do now was hold his peace and wait.

"You know," Kenny said, his expression opening to the concept, "that might not be a bad idea. You always been good with numbers, and ran J&H Grocery like a champ. Made some pretty good suggestions around here that helped a lot, too."

Lem's heartbeat quickened and a sense of pride pulsed through his veins. "Yeah, I did all right by the store. The few suggestions I made about the operations in here was just common sense."

"You been a solid entrepreneur all your life; just had the wrong product to start out with. But even with that, wrong as it might have been, you do have a good head on your shoulders—always have."

"I feel you . . . but do you think I could really be all that if another opportunity presented itself?"

"I think so. No, let me say it plain—I know so, brother." Kenny neared him and slapped his shoulder again.

A sense of satisfaction settled in Lem's bones. "I'ma try to be up for the challenge, Kenny—if opportunity knocks. That's why I went around to the Center . . . trying to get a feel for it, to see if that could be for me, you know?"

"Yeah. I do know."

Kenny's tone was encouraging, and his expression was so honest that Lem wanted to just spit it out and really tell the man what was on his mind, but something in his gut held him back.

"Well, one day, I might go back and get some basics. Who knows?"

"That'd be cool," Kenny told him as the telephones began to ring. "Man, I gotta get somebody in here to open up before nine—this seven A.M. start-time is kicking my natural ass. I knew you'd always have my back."

"Yeah," Lem said quietly, slowly understanding that Kenny assumed anything he learned would be put into the towing company, not his own separate venture. He also sadly realized that everything he'd just told Kenny would only remain cool if it would benefit Chadway Towing.

Lem studied his friend as Kenny took a tow job and thrust the information on a piece of paper toward Lem. Maxine wasn't the only one who had trouble in getting Kenny to see beyond his business, but then again, he couldn't blame the man. One day, when he'd have his own, he'd probably be the same way. He too would be all-consumed, focused on success, and trying with all his might to build something secure and permanent for his family. That was what a man was supposed to do.

But right now, all he could do was glance at his mentor and slip quietly out the door.

four

Jem pulled up to the Chadway house and peeped over his shoulder at his son, who was busily chewing on a rubber pretzel toy in the car seat. The certified bank check in his pocket for three thousand dollars weighed heavily. He let his breath out hard and gripped the steering wheel. His nerves were shot. Bird had no basis of an argument, he told himself, if she ever found out about the check. Hell, she had bought a brand-new car without asking him first. Truth. So, he should have the right to take fifteen hundred dollars out of the joint account for something more important than a new ride, and it should also be his right to use some of his overtime money for something he'd worked hard for. She'd just have to deal with it when it all came out in the wash.

He studied his brother-in-law's home with new eyes as he gathered his energy and thoughts. This was what he wanted to do for his wife and baby boy one day. Of course, she'd understand that he needed earnest money to even begin the negotiation to take the building off the market. Yet if everything was so cool and so logical, then why was he a basket case at the moment?

"Come on, little man," he said to Jay, who responded with a drooling gurgle as Lem slipped out of the driver's seat and opened the back door to fetch him.

Yeah, there was no reason to be on edge. He was trippin'. All he could reason was that the long week of secretly practicing his presentation in the bathroom mirror hadn't helped. Nor had rushing back and forth to the Center between tows in order to review his work a hundred times. Tonight he had to do a dry run in front of the other members of his class. And their opinions mattered.

If he couldn't get it right in front of a friendly crowd, then what was it going to be like with the Center board members there? Not to mention, what was his wife's reaction going to be? He prayed to God that Bird would just be cool—that she would pump him up if things didn't go according to plan and he messed up, and better yet, that she would be ecstatic if he did well. The entire process gave him a whole new appreciation for struggling entertainers trying to make it at the Apollo. He closed his eyes briefly and opened them, taking in another steadying breath. He'd never laugh at an artist who was bombing on stage or television again!

"Let's go see Aunt Maxine, huh? How about that?" Lem hoisted Jay up into his arms and approached the door.

As the doorbell sounded, he could hear the normal

clamor of family commotion while he waited on the porch.

"Hey, Uncle Lem. Whassup?"

Lem pounded his nephew's fist. "You, brother," he said with a grin, and then cuffed Ahmad's shoulder.

"Uncle Lem!"

"How's my favorite number two girl?" Lem leaned down to kiss his niece, Kelly, balancing Jay to reach her upturned face.

"How come I'm not number one?"

Lem laughed. " 'Cause your Aunt Bird is number one. You been a good girl and been helping Mommy?"

"I help all the time," she said proudly. "Ahmad doesn't do his chores, though."

"Oh, be quiet. Uncle Lem, she's always getting on my nerves, you know what I mean?"

Lem gave Ahmad a wink as he made his way to the kitchen. "Y'all do your homework," he called over his shoulder, leaving the two squabbling youngsters to verbally battle it out.

Stepping through the archway, he smiled as his newest niece sat on the floor banging a pot with a wooden spoon. "There's my number three favorite girl—the drummer."

His sister-in-law turned around, smiled, and pulled a dishtowel off her shoulder. As she put a hand on her slender hip, he looked at the tall, graceful woman before him, wondering how Kenny could keep up arguments with her? Maxine was pretty, smart, and genuine. A more mellow, taller, and leaner version of his cocoa brown Bird, with Nubian locks.

"Hey, Lem . . . and how's my baby boy," Maxine cooed, immediately reaching for Jay, who went right to her. "Who's your favorite auntie? I've got a cookie for my little man. Let's get that coat and hat off so you can bang pots, too."

Lem took in the mouthwatering smells and the happy chaos in Maxine's sanctuary, her kitchen. One day. One day . . .

"I really appreciate you watching Jay tonight, Maxine. Like I told you on the phone, Bird got hung up at the salon, and I have my volunteer thing to do tonight. Just this one more Wednesday, and we won't have to bug you guys during the week too much after that. She'll probably be by to get Jay, 'cause I might be later than anticipated."

His gaze slid from Maxine's. He wished he could just tell somebody in the family what was going on. The secret was burning him like an unopened Christmas present, but he let out a long breath instead of words.

Maxine gave him a brief glance as though she knew he had something more to say, but was cool enough to wait for him to tell it on his own.

"It is never a problem for me to watch my nephew, Lem. You go do what you gotta do. He'll be fine, and we'll all eat as soon as Kenny gets in. If you two get hung up real late, I'll put him in bed and you all can pick him up in the morning like always."

Maxine's words flowed over him like balm. Drawn by sheer affection, he stepped toward her and pecked her on the cheek.

For Better, For Worse 75

"Thanks, Sis. I needed to hear that tonight."

She hoisted his son down next to his niece, removing the child's outer layers of clothing and tossing them onto an empty kitchen chair. She then handed Jay a wooden spoon so he could join in the pot-banging band. Her easy countenance and mellow voice was a gift. Kenny needed to take note. Maxine was an angel. She smiled at the youngsters as she stood up. The two little ones giggled in delight as they tried to out-noise each other. Satisfied that she'd found something to momentarily occupy them while she went back to the task of preparing dinner, Maxine collected her dishtowel and slung it over her shoulder again.

"You seem like you're really committed to this volunteering, Lem. That's really, really positive. I'm proud of you."

A slight pang of guilt made his response come slowly. He and Maxine had always seen eye to eye. Which was even cooler, since Kenny was his boy. If Kenny were married to Teri, their man-to-man friendship would have suffered from the get-go. But Maxine was nice—his favorite of Bird's sisters, even though she and Bird bickered like it didn't make sense. Why Bird listened more to Teri than Maxine was beyond him.

"Thanks, Max," he replied quietly after a moment. "I just wish Bird could understand that I need something for me . . . something beyond the day-to-day grind that we all have to do to pay the bills."

God had to understand that he would never want to destabilize this home. It was too precious, too warm, and it had too much love. But he needed a sanctuary like this for him and Bird and Jay, too. Tension began creeping back into his body.

"I can relate," Maxine said with a sigh. She leaned against the sink, folding her arms over her chest. "Sometimes you just need something to nourish your soul along the way. Bird has, and loves her salon. A little volunteering doesn't seem like too much to ask."

The two nodded, drifting in their own private dilemmas.

"How's the writing going?" His question was partly motivated as a diversion from the thoughts clanging about in his brain. Maybe Maxine had the magic answer about how to get Kenny to accept change.

Her initial answer was a long exhalation.

"Okay," she finally said, then turned from him to wash vegetables in the sink.

"Just okay?" He pressed for some reason, not exactly sure why.

"Don't get me wrong," she said in a dejected tone. "I love writing, especially the poetry and short stories, but it kicks up a lot of static in here."

"Aw, c'mon, Max. Why is that? It's just sitting quietly to—"

"Do you hear quiet in here?" Maxine offered him a sad laugh and turned around to face him again. "My day is filled with running errands, doing fifty things that Kenny doesn't have time to do, and participating in the school activities for the kids—with a baby on my hip. Then, after they all get home, you see this chaos. After dinner, I've got to fight with people to get their homework done, pack lunches, listen to Kenny's day, and then, if there's any quiet time left, that's Kenny's time of mine that he claims. Not that I'm complaining; he works hard and needs me to be his sounding board. He's a good man . . . a good husband and father."

Lem didn't say a word, or even dare blink. This was Kenny's house, and he was hearing a confession that he wasn't sure he should be hearing. It was all in Maxine's tone, which was still half-cheerful, but somewhat resigned. He tucked away the knowledge of what else might be resident in the sound of her voice—wistfulness to do her own thing.

After a moment, she picked up where she left off, as though speaking to herself. "I hear all about his day, the issues at the company. And after I do all that, if I still have enough energy left to jot down some thoughts before going to bed, your brother-in-law makes it hard to keep my focus on my work." She chuckled and briefly glanced away. "So, the writing is going as well as can be expected, under the circumstances."

"Damn . . ." Lem's response trailed off as he leaned against the kitchen doorframe and smoothed his beard with his palm. "Complex, no doubt."

"Yeah. Complex."

"I feel bad now for adding to the mayhem by dropping Jay off on you—I just didn't know."

"No, don't you even go there, Lem," she corrected. "This doesn't have a thing to do with you. In fact, just knowing that somebody in the family is making positive strides for themselves, I wanted to support that. Me and Kenny are all right—we go through our little silent struggles from time to time, which never amount to much . . . just a part of being married." Her smile was broad and warm as she studied him with an affectionate glance. "So, you go on and volunteer. I'll be fine."

"But, Max, seriously. I understand the family support vibe, and we should all stick together for better or worse, and under emergency circumstances—but each person should also have something that feeds their soul, you know?"

Lem pushed himself away from the doorframe and began pacing as Maxine stared at him. "It's like, synergy. The family is the whole, strengthened by the parts. But each part has to have its own strength, its own special value to bring to the whole. And that needs to be appreciated both individually and collectively. Am I making sense?"

"Too much sense, Lem." Maxine walked over to the toddlers on the floor, stooped down, and handed each one a cookie. "I'm gonna start calling you Socrates, brother-in-law. You're the philosopher, these days. You go, boy."

Her compliment grew roots, making him bolder. "Maxine, listen. I know Kenny is a hard sell, and he can be as stubborn as a mule—much as we all love our brother. But keep working on him. I mean . . . you could start mailing out your finished pieces to some women's magazines, see if your poems and short stories get picked up somewhere, all for the cost of a stamp."

Everything he'd absorbed in class rushed into his mind. He scavenged bits of information that he'd learned from his talks with his peers, the diverse group of entrepreneurs with whom he communed every Wednesday, and remembered that one sister had done that. Why couldn't Maxine?

When Maxine didn't immediately answer, but tucked a stray lock back into her ponytail scrunchie, he knew she was giving his suggestion consideration. Nobody should have their spirit squashed and their dreams derailed. There was certainly enough room in the Chadway household for a creative soul like Maxine to try her thing—especially when it was such a positive endeavor.

"Look," he pressed on, not wanting to allow her, or anybody, to give in to defeat. "You could make copies of your work during the day at the copy center while running errands, at like eight cents each. No serious investment."

"Yeah," she said slowly. "I could do that. But what if I mail all my stuff out and somebody jacks it? I'd die if I saw my work in a magazine under somebody else's name."

"Then copyright it," he quickly replied. "You can do that one of two ways. Either mail it to yourself and don't break the seal—that's a poor man's copyright. Or send for an application: it costs like thirty to forty bucks, it's one easy page, and you can get the app from the U.S. Copyright and Patent Office in D.C. Or go on the Internet, Max, and download the form. It ain't hard."

"Okay," Maxine said with a deep chuckle, folding her arms over her chest again and looking at him without blinking. "Now I'm scared, because you are blowing me away. Where'd you learn all this?"

That he could teach her something legitimate that she didn't already know sent a shot of pride through him, and he seized upon the feeling like a man grabbing for a life raft.

"I've been down at the Center for twelve weeks, Maxine. The people there, and the knowledge they drop in their small business classes, are awesome."

He checked his enthusiasm and went on more slowly. "You learn a lot just hanging around people who know more than you do, and I've been picking up stuff I never dreamed of. That's why I love going there. It flexes a part of my mind that hasn't been tapped lately. I mean, I always had the ability, but nothing to practice on. That's what I'm trying to tell you. Don't give up, just work it into your situation peacefully, and hopefully, sooner or later, the other members of the family will have your back."

Her face beamed with barely contained excitement and her fingers went to her lips for a moment before she spoke. "When I was at Kenny's business, I found out that I could do something other than run a house. Not that I don't love my children and family . . . but I was really good at it, Lem. But that caused static, so I backed off. Chadway Towing is Kenny's domain, and he wasn't trying to share it. Then, I almost won that political campaign. I was good at that, too; really, really good at organizing. But you know how that went—I lost. So, I left it alone. But I started keeping a journal, writing down my thoughts, feelings, hopes.... Writing is so personal, Lem. I just want to try it."

"Then try it, Max."

The two held each other's gaze for a moment.

"I wanted to take a few writing classes at night, but I knew that Kenny would have a fit. He'd be all evil and cranky if he came home from work and had to deal with the kids by himself. Been there, seen it, done it. I can't ask Teri to step in, because she already did time at the Chadway ranch when Kenny was recovering from the car accident, just like you did. And Bird is just really getting back to herself after her own recovery from that accident, and has to get the salon rolling strong... I guess everybody is trying to get back on their feet with their own thing."

"Okay," Lem conceded. "Then take it in baby steps. First try to polish what you've got, and start a mailing campaign. You did that when you were running for public office, right?"

Maxine laughed. "Sure did. Turned my kitchen table into a post office and a campaign headquarters."

"Well, then?"

"We'll see," she hedged, coming up to him to give him a hug. "Thanks, Lem, for listening to me vent. Just knowing that somebody in this family understands makes all the difference in the world."

"I hear you," he replied, returning her hug and pulling back to look at her. "Just knowing that somebody believes in you definitely makes a difference—

even if things don't work out like you wanted, at least they were in your cheering section while you tried."

"I'll talk to Bird. Okay?" Maxine touched his cheek and made her way over to the stove.

How did women know things without words having to tell them, he wondered? It was definitely a psychic gift. "Thanks, Max."

"I know my sister is over there giving you the blues because she thinks every waking moment of yours should be spent making love to her." Maxine laughed in an easy, nonjudgmental tone. "Bird is the youngest, spoiled rotten, and a trip. But she loves you, Lem. She'll come around, just like Kenny will, I suppose."

A battle over the television in the next room drew their attention away for a moment.

"Nobody should be fighting over what show they're not supposed to watch until the table is set, and all homework is done," Maxine hollered.

A disgruntled series of "yes, ma'ams" followed her command. Lem checked his watch.

"You want something to eat before you run?"

Maxine's offer was tempting, but he had whiled away enough time and had to roll.

"Naw. I really gotta go."

She went to the top of the refrigerator, pulling down a loaf of bread and taking out two slices. "I'm going to put a piece of fried fish in some foil with hot sauce on it, and you can take one of the kids' juice boxes to go with it. Eat in the car on your way, so you can think—and bring me back some more knowledge from your class, Socrates."

"Deal," he said with a smile, accepting all the gifts his sister-in-law had bestowed upon him.

"I told you that acquiring the building wouldn't be the primary problem," Linda Maxwell told the group of somber consultants that sat around the table. They had serious business to discuss before any of the Center's students arrived. "The owners, after hardball negotiation, agreed to take back the mortgage under the following conditions: one, they want the building to revert back to them immediately, without a sheriff sale process, if the payments lapse more than one hundred and twenty days. Which means as soon as our client's construction gets completed, he's got to be ready to hit the ground running with his shops—or else the owners just got themselves a newly renovated space for free."

Linda flipped a page on her legal pad. No one spoke, and it was as though they were all saying a private prayer for a miracle.

"I also got a letter of intent from our sister agency to rent out the after-school space, with a contingency agreement that they will only rent it if the timing is right, with a September readiness date so they can be in there when the new school year commences, and if the computer equipment and furnishings are in place. Which all means that this thing has to meet deadlines. However, we've gotten our first rental agreement in principle, and that will help Russell work with the financial institutions."

"The letter of intent to occupy will definitely help

our finance coach do his thing. But the mortgage stipulations represent some serious risk," Iola Carter remarked in a concerned tone. "What else, Linda? Our client is coming in here tonight, and I want us to have as much of this hammered out beforehand, so he doesn't lose confidence."

Linda Maxwell nodded, studying her yellow legal pad as she spoke. "Number two, they are willing to give Lem Van Adams a one-year grace period on the start of mortgage payments, which he'll need to secure the financing and to get the construction completed."

"But?" Russell Hampton chimed in.

"But, that option to find and secure financing is only good for four months. They reason that if it takes longer than four months to get this project financed, then the construction, which will take six to eight months, could run over the grace period. We all know that Lem's getting financing is not a foregone conclusion."

"That's tight." The Center's finance coach sighed.

"Yeah." Linda pushed back her chair and put the end of her pen into her mouth, chewing on it. "That's a lot of risk."

"The board is not going to go for the 504 program financing—whereby our organization funds forty percent and the banks do fifty percent—on a building that could revert back to the owners once renovated." Russell Hampton made a tent with his fingers and leaned forward. "The financial institutions will want something tangible to assure that this client won't be left holding the bag, thereby leaving them free-falling with a two-hundred-and-twenty-five-thousand-dollar loan attached to an asset that they have no position on. That won't work."

"The owners take second position on the structure—that much I did get," Linda countered. "After renovations, the property could bring a market price of at least a half million. The financial institutions would take first position on it as collateral."

"Okay, you're making me feel better. Slightly," Russell said.

"Damn, Linda," Iola exclaimed, letting her breath out in a rush of relief. "How'd you swing that?"

"By hardballing their consciences, and bringing in community group letters of support for the agency and its client. But you should know that the politicians wouldn't touch this with a ten-foot pole, because of Van Adams's past. Let this thing get renovated without a hitch, and they'll be the first ones there, battling for the scissors to cut the ribbon. But let there be any question about this client's financing sources, or the types of businesses run through this establishment, and they will bring the torches to burn him at the stake—with news cameras in tow. And you are aware of why our board members are so positively freaked out by this project. It could jeopardize our future funding if a scandal ever got attached to this, and by extension, our agency. Van Adams doesn't just have to walk the chalk line on this project; the man better do back flips on it."

"Which leads me to the points that nobody ever wants to thoroughly discuss in front of our client,

Iola." Russell Hampton turned his attention to the lead instructor and let his breath out hard.

"It's now or never, Russell. Shoot."

"I know you really believe in this client, as do all of us." He paused, his gaze stopping at each concerned face at the table. "I want this brother to get this chance as much as anybody. But the banks are really balking about his past criminal record. It could be the showstopper."

"He's got to have a chance, though," Iola whispered. "The man served his time, and has shown people that he's straight now. Russell, can't you do something? Just tell us."

Linda Maxwell briefly closed her eyes, then picked up her black-framed reading glasses as her shoulders sagged. "This one's a heartbreaker, Iola. A goddamned Catch-22." She shook her head as she put on her glasses, her tone becoming strident. "They want the brothers to do the right thing, and then block access to that at every turn. Here we have a perfectly plausible business plan, a couple that has enough assets to make this thing fly with low risk, a man with the capacity to do it—and we're hitting brick walls at every turn for him." Her voice wavered with repressed emotion as she snatched off her glasses again and tossed them onto the table with a rattle.

"I'm not a miracle worker, folks," Russell said calmly. Strain was etched across his face as he tried to make the group understand. "The dynamics are simple. Strike one: Van Adams has no formal education. We do not have an MBA graduate making the request."

"But what about all of his experience in managing a family business?" Now Iola Carter was standing and pacing. "His education may not have taken the conventional route, but he has more of a track record at managing huge amounts of money and responsibility than some wet-behind-the-ears MBA!"

"Hear me out, Iola. As the agency lead instructor and Center director, you know this project is bigger than a micro-loan to open a barbershop, or to start a little catering business. Van Adams came in here with a serious vision."

"I know," she murmured, holding on to the back of her chair with her eyes closed. "I know."

"Strike two: his age. He is under thirty and asking for two hundred and twenty-five thousand dollars. He's not forty years old with a longer management track record to mitigate his past, so to speak. If he had twenty years between his past and now, it would still be a stretch. But that would have helped our case for him." Russell Hampton worked the muscles in his shoulders.

"This man does not have a credit record to show that he's ever borrowed this much before, or repaid it. He has assets via his joint marital holdings, but nothing on his own, in his name alone. If he had a home that he'd purchased alone, or something else . . . But our client does not have collateral—except the collateral that we'll be able to show from the salon, their cars, their portion of the family home they live in, and the project building itself. While all of that is substantial, and covers all the exposure on this project, he wants to try to keep his joint resources off the table—and we really can't. We need Mrs. Van Adams to give him credibility at this juncture, no matter how Van Adams feels about that. He won't have a prayer without her in the equation, and even then..." Russell Hampton's voice trailed off.

"Once again, we're back to strike three," Iola Carter whispered. "He's been incarcerated."

"Fucking ball game," Linda exclaimed, throwing her pen across the desk in frustration. "And we're insane, because we knew that going in."

"I'm still not willing to give up," Iola said. Her knuckles turned white as she gripped her chair. "This man has repaid his societal debt, he has potential, and he can do this. He's bringing us three grand tonight to hold that building with whatever agreement Linda has cooked up. He's been at every class, offered insight, participated fully—and dammit, I just can't watch another brother get thrown back into the system meat grinder to be chopped up into little pieces. That's why we are here as an agency. That's why we all left cushy corporate jobs: to be able to help people. That's our freakin' agency mission—to give people who missed their first shot a second shot."

"You're preaching to the choir, Iola," Russell replied gently.

"The system isn't designed to give out *big* second chances, Iola, and you know that," Linda argued. "People can get themselves together to cut hair, bake sweet potato pies, or sell incense on the corner—but they will not be allowed to do a Michael Millken.

Namely, go to jail and come out to make another fortune. Enron Corporation execs can do it, but not a brother from the hood. We have to be real and cope with the double standard before we jack up this client's head, if we haven't already."

"That's why we *need* to do this one case, to demonstrate what can be done within the economic development community. *Just one, to show them all.* I'm not trying to replace five-dollar-an-hour wages at a fast food joint with eight-dollar-an-hour small businesses. I want to build real, lasting *wealth* in our community. Take people to the next level." Iola sat down in her chair hard. "Aren't you all tired of this shit?"

"Yeah, we all are," Russell replied calmly. "All right. We start trying to work miracles. Linda, if those are the terms the owner will offer, then that's what we'll take. Step one, secure the building."

Iola Carter let out her breath with relief again, and swallowed hard.

"So let's review his sources for collateral," Russell continued.

Iola took her time answering him. "His wife has a beauty salon worth probably one-fifty, as we know, and I understand that his brother-in-law owns a towing business, and the Van Adams's are one-third owners of a solid, single-family home. He will not even broach this with extended family, but his wife might go for it. And our client said that his wife would definitely let him use the salon."

Linda laughed and retrieved her cast-off pen with a smile. "Thank you, God!"

"But . . . er . . . Houston, there's a problem," Iola said, watching the sudden relief on her colleagues' faces become eclipsed with worry again. "His wife doesn't know that he's been coming here all these weeks. He wants to surprise her at the graduation."

"Oh . . . shit . . ." Linda lowered her head to the table. "You mean to tell us that's why he's been so cagey about letting us run the numbers with the joint marital property all these weeks? Lord, have mercy . . ." She pushed herself up and looked at Iola. "Tell him to tell his wife before graduation. Period."

"He wanted to do this himself. His pride is at—"

"My grandmother told me that pride goeth before a fall, Iola." Russell looked at her hard. "Now, I am not Houdini, although I've got this brother's back. He's going to have to use the salon as collateral—that's the bottom line. If the salon is worth one-fifty and the building self-collateralizes at one-fifty before renovations, we can more than show the financial institutions that their exposure is covered. He'll also have to supply twenty-five thousand in cash from honest sources. I take it those monies are in a joint account, and he'll need clearance from the other owners of his primary residence to pledge that, too. So our good brother had better handle his family business, or this is just a pipe dream, where all of us have been wasting our time. And then we've still gotta light a candle and say a prayer that that works."

"I'll talk to him tonight," Iola promised. "Maybe his wife will support him, even if the other people in his family won't."

"You'd better put on your marriage counseling hat, Iola," Linda said, shaking her head. "This kind of thing never goes according to Hoyle."

"I'll try to get a community development financial institution to sit at the table with the banks, because they are a little more flexible—given that community investment is their mantra. They've seen this stuff before, or at least had it pitched to them. If a CDFI steps in to share the risk, then maybe we can pull this off. But I'm going to need the salon, Iola," Russell Hampton said firmly. "The salon gives me more than collateral—it gives me a six-figure business that I can show the client had management involvement with, so I can give the brother a little more yeast in his skill résumé."

"You'd better work it, Mr. H," Iola chuckled with relief. "You'd better work it."

"So, twenty-five Gs, people?" Linda's question hung in the air.

"Okay, back to square one. He has to get his wife to give that up from joint savings, too. It's the ten percent minimum equity that has to be cash or a liquid asset, and has to come from trackable, honest sources—like the salon, or another credible, aboveboard investor. This cannot be three-card-monte dollars. This is cold cash that the financial people will want to see at the table when it's time to go to settlement. So, our client better kiss and make up with his wife, and be real nice to her."

The group looked at Russell Hampton and nodded their agreement.

* * *

Time and Heaven were messin' with him. Time had dragged its ass all week, making every minute pass with excruciating slowness. Then all of a sudden, *bam!* Wednesday had rolled around again. But the day had crawled by like a turtle. Now it was sprinting like a jackrabbit, and his wife was slowing around and dawdling. He was about to jump out of his skin.

"C'mon, Bird!" Lem walked in a circle as he mentally recited his presentation. Why the hell did it take women so long to get dressed?

"Hold your horses," she fussed. "You got me running in from the salon, jumping through a shower, and putting on some church-looking, plain, long black dress—with pearls from Teri, no less, like my silver hoops weren't good enough, while you put on some navy blue suit and white shirt funeral gear. Then, I couldn't even half feed my baby before you were scooping him up and rushing him over to my sister's house; now I can't even get my makeup on good and—"

"Please, Bird. I have to be on time! I'm giving a part of the presentation."

She stopped applying lipstick in the mirror and looked at him. "You didn't tell me you were one of the graduation presenters. That's nice, Lem. Wow. Those people must really think you're a good instructor. I'm proud of you."

"I told you I was doing a little part before," he grumbled. "But you don't listen to me."

"You did. I forgot. My bad. But, I *am* proud of you, though."

Her words felt as good as a hug, and helped remove the immediate adrenaline rush of irritation he'd felt when she told him that she'd forgotten he was a part of the graduation ceremony. "You think I look okay? My suit cool?"

"You look fine," she said softly, coming to him and brushing off his lapels. "I can finish this up in the car. We don't want you to be late."

Twenty-five nerve-shattering minutes passed between them without a word in the car. Occasionally his wife glanced at him from the corner of her eye as she touched up her makeup and fidgeted with her hair and the radio. His focus was singular: the presentation. As they neared the graduation site, every fear in the world began crawling through his bloodstream like a virus.

Iola Carter had made it plain last week. The agency and all the instructors had stepped out on faith for him; they'd done all they could do. Now it was up to him to sell himself, as well as his dream. He knew the risks, nothing was guaranteed. There would be board members there, a couple of bankers who might be potential backers, and a community development financial institution. All of his peers from class and their families would either see him fly, or crash and burn. Each of the top five class candidates had fifteen minutes of fame, and he'd drawn the unlucky lottery position of presenting last.

But, "The first shall be last and the last shall be first." Momma Joe had told him that from the Bible, once. *God in Heaven, hear my prayer.* He should have told his wife that he'd revised his proposal to include her shop and their portion of the Joseph home as collateral. He should have explained to Iola Carter that he still hadn't spoken to Bird about this change yet, despite his promise to do so. There would be small talk, wine and cheese before they started. He shoulda explained to Bird about needing to dredge their accounts, too, in order to do this deal. It wasn't the kind of conversation to have on a casual basis in public; he knew better. What had he been thinking? The board members might say something to his wife—who might go off before he'd even gotten a chance to take the podium in the large multipurpose room.

Then afterward, there would be a cake, certificates handed out, families and friends all laughing and talking—and his wife might be ornery and not having any of it. She might start a public argument. *God hear my prayer.*

Lem blotted the moisture from his forehead with the back of his hand.

"It's going to be all right, baby," his wife's gentle voice reassured him.

"I've never done anything like this before, Bird," he replied, trying to infuse his words with energy, hoping she'd believe him, needing her to trust him. Needing her to know that he wasn't just talking about a presentation, either.

"All you have to do is say a few words of encouragement and step down. You'll be fine. I'm so proud. I just wish Maxine and Kenny and Teri could see you.

For Better, For Worse 95

We should have brought the kids, too. We would have all come to support you. Why didn't you give everybody enough notice so we all could have been here for you tonight?"

"Woulda made me more nervous," he admitted. "I just wanted you there, in case things didn't go as planned." His mouth went dry. If he messed up, at least the entire family wouldn't witness his failure. "No matter how I do, honey, or what I say up there . . . I just need you to believe in me, okay?"

"Of course, Lem. Why wouldn't I?"

"I don't know . . ." He spotted a parking space and whipped the car into it quickly. "I look okay, though, right?"

Bird chuckled as he jumped out of the car, started walking, and then hurried back to open the car door for her.

As she followed her husband to the massive glass doors, she appraised the downtown high-rise. The bitter fall wind whipped at her hair and the hem of her coat, pushing her toward the building. A sudden pang of insecurity sneaked into her mind when she glimpsed herself in the chrome reflection of the elevator doors in the grand lobby.

No wonder Lem was nervous. Bird carefully patted her hair into place, lifting parts of it with her fingers and using the elevator doors as a mirror. This was one of those top-notch joints that Teri worked in, and she didn't feel adequately dressed for the occasion, despite the black dress and pearls. Had Lem told her that the graduation was being held in a special location downtown, and not at the Center in the community, she might have bumped up her program a level. Now it was her turn to fight the butterflies.

"You coulda told a sister that they were doing this graduation thing to the nines, instead of letting me fall in here like some old housewife going to church."

"You look fine, Bird," he assured her, without glancing at her. "They needed a place big enough to hold all the students and their guests."

"Deep. How many people you think will be there that you have to speak in front of?"

"I don't know." He breathed out hard. "Fifty to sixty people, maybe."

"Deep," she murmured again.

Other neatly dressed, nervous-looking couples with families tagging along joined them in the elevator. On the ride up, Lem broke the ice and introduced them to his wife, exchanging pleasantries. When the doors opened on the twenty-seventh floor, Lem took in a deep breath through his nose and let it slowly filter out. It was show time. He ushered Bird out on his arm, quickly glancing around the room to find his instructors.

Each of the Center coaches was mingling with clients and board members. An array of cut vegetables and dips had been set up in the wood-paneled lobby, and men in waiters' black-and-white uniforms butlered wine, small bottled waters, and miniature soft drinks. If this was how the high-rollers rolled . . . if this was what Teri was accustomed to, then damn . . . no wonder he wasn't worth squat in her eyes.

"This is *all that*, Lem," his wife whispered as he helped her out of her coat and then removed his own. "These were the people you were teaching with all these weeks? Damn, I'm impressed. Where are the kids? There's a lot of parents here . . . are the young folks gonna wear caps and gowns, and going to come in all at one time?"

"Let me check these in the closet," Lem said, evading Bird's questions, "and you grab something to eat. I'll find one of the instructors and try to get the lowdown. Cool?"

"Okay," she cheerfully replied, then eased into the group by the food tables.

He'd noticed that Bird had taken her time, though. She was clearly impressed at the level of people he'd been around for twelve weeks, but that also seemed to make her just a little jittery.

"Hey, man!" One of Lem's classmates came up to him and offered him a hearty handshake. "They pulled out the stops for us, didn't they? The twelve weeks was worth it. Come on over and meet my mom."

"Cool," Lem said slowly, his gaze trained on Iola Carter as he walked. The sister was working the hell out of the room—as were the other coaches. Every face that wasn't brown or young was one that he knew he had to impress.

Making cursory conversation with his fellow classmates, he made his way through the throng, avoiding Bird and trying to get within the networking zone—near his instructors.

"Mr. Van Adams," Iola Carter said in an ebullient voice. "Meet some members from our board." She opened the circle and let Lem step in.

"We've been hearing only the best things about you," one board member said.

Names collided against Lem's brain as Iola Carter introduced a series of board members in a single breath. How in the world did she do that? She was definitely a pro. He tried to remember who was who, what position they held, and also what was in his presentation, all at the same time.

"Van Adams has an excellent vision," Linda Maxwell added as she stepped into the small power circle. His legal coach beamed at him. "In all my years of community economic development, I've never seen anyone with as much promise."

"And so I've heard, from multiple sources tonight," one of the bankers in the group said. "Russell Hampton has been slaying me with your revenue projections, Mr. Van Adams," he added, extending his hand to Lem. "We can't wait to see what you've got."

From the corner of his eye, he saw Bird approaching. She held a small plate in one hand and was casually munching on cheese as she walked toward them. *Not now!* The thought leapt into his mind. It wasn't about being ashamed of her, it was that he was working it, and needed no derailments from a misplaced comment from her. His nerves frayed as she came closer. He should have talked to Bird before this. Too late now.

"I'd like to introduce you to my lovely wife," Lem said coolly, drawing a brilliant smile of pride from

Bird, as she quickly popped a cheese square back onto her plate and shook everyone's hand.

"We have heard so much about the salon and your plans for expansion," an older, female board member said. "It is wonderful to have women in business, especially in the African-American community that so desperately needs the economic boost. Claire McFarland—board president. Welcome."

The woman extended her hand, and Bird tentatively accepted it.

"Well, thank you," Bird said with caution, her smile still there as she withdrew her palm from the woman's hand. "I'm so proud that my husband would think to mention it to you. It was just a little dream of mine that we've kicked around from time to time. Maybe one day."

He could tell that his wife had switched gears and was playing it to the bone. Bird was no dummy. She knew how this all went. The smile she gave now was her business smile, not the thousand-watter reserved for family and friends. Cool. And the board member's comment could have been taken in two ways. But he didn't want to push his luck.

"I'd like you to meet the Center coaches, too, honey: Iola Carter, director and marketing specialist; Russell Hampton, finance expert; Linda Maxwell, legal counsel. Please excuse us, folks; I'd like to introduce my wife to some of the interns, too."

"I don't have anything in my teeth, do I?" Bird whispered as Lem turned away from the circle toward other guests.

"You're cool, baby. Everything is cool. Just work it."

Lem's gaze locked with Iola Carter's as he passed her. *I haven't told her. Bird doesn't know.*

"It's going to be wonderful to listen to the presentations tonight," Iola Carter said to everyone. "Maybe we should get started, and all be surprised by the excellence and hard work that went into what we have in store for you."

The board members nodded, smiled, agreed and began to disperse. Iola Carter had obviously heard his unspoken plea for assistance. There was a God in Heaven. His wife was squeezing his arm in support and he hoped Iola's words would cue her in that surprises were coming. Iola Carter could apparently read minds, eye contact, and pick up scared-shitless on radar.

It was *definitely* show time. He rubbed Bird's arm for good luck.

five

Her butt was getting sore from sitting so long. Bird glanced at her husband, whose expression was stone serious. Lem's eyes were focused on the people who were going through fancy presentations. By now she'd gathered that they were *in* the class, and were doing these mock presentations. Lem was a trip. He could have told her he was taking a class. But she had to admit that she was proud of him for trying to better himself. Whatever he had learned would surely help Kenny in his business, so it was all good. She'd give her husband a little attitude about his flimflam excuse for where he was, for lying. But this was definitely a positive place for him to be, all things considered.

She *was* hungry, though—that cheese and dip stuff wasn't real food. This was worse than church. At least you got to hear good preaching and got to hear some slammin' music at Victory Bible AME. Plus, after it was all said and done, they fed you.

It had been hard enough to listen to each one of the boring Center coaches, as they explained the program mission statement and the history of the organization. Then she'd had to suffer some woman drone on about the need for self-empowerment. When were they going to get to the end, where the students got their certificates, and she and Lem could jet?

Bird fidgeted in her chair and let out a sigh of impatience. "When do you go on, baby? I'm hungry."

Lem shushed her, and she settled back into her seat, disgruntled. Men.

Finally the woman who reminded her of her sister Teri stood up, while people clapped. As the sister-look-alike made her way to the podium, Bird surveyed her with suspicion. Maybe this was what really had Lem coming out to the Center every Wednesday night. She'd kick his ass if there was anything shaky going down.

"Now, for our final presentation of the evening before we present certificates." The woman beamed.

Bird noted that the muscles in Lem's legs and arms had constricted, and he leaned forward. Oh, yeah. She was definitely watching this bitch.

"The next presentation is by far the most visionary one that this Center has seen in a long time. It gives me the greatest pleasure to introduce Mr. Lem Van Adams."

Momentary confusion hit her as she watched her husband stand tall and make his way to the front of the room. She'd thought he was just going to do part of the certificate handoff and make a little speech, not be doing a whole presentation like the others. Deep. Very, very deep. Bird's body moved toward the edge of her chair.

She studied his proud carriage and her gaze swept the line of important people who sat at a long table that took up the front row like a judging bench. What was going on? From the way they craned their necks and leaned forward with little pads before them, she knew somehow that her man was in some sort of competition. Maybe for top honors in the class, or something? Wow. If she could just see their faces, instead of the backs of their heads. . . .

"Good evening. Thank you all for coming out to support our entrepreneurial objectives."

That could not be her husband throwing around big words. His voice was eloquent, smooth, controlled. And damn, he looked good! Her focus riveted on the man who'd taken over Lem's body as he deftly clipped on a small microphone, picked up a laser pointer, and manipulated colorful slides for the group while he spoke.

She could not comprehend the transformation.

He was talking about a building . . . a building with their last name on it! Every nerve ending in her body went on red alert. He described a neighborhood, walked the floor as he talked, motioning with his hands better than their minister, Reverend Pryor. The man was awesome as he spat out polysyllables. Electricity pulsed through Bird, making her fingertips tingle. She rubbed her palms down her thighs to rid them of moisture. Her baby was *on.* He was in control. He sounded like one of them high-roller financiers. Her baby was Wall Street—*goddamn.*

Lem walked over to an easel and turned it around

to face the crowd. A low murmur of approval zigzagged through the audience. Bird covered her mouth with one hand. *Oh my God . . .*

He calmly strode back to the podium, leaned forward, and made a request for two-hundred-and-twenty-five what . . . ? She could not breathe. Even in the mock presentation, it sure sounded convincing. His hand flipped another slide with the remote. A red laser light hit the screen. All of their assets and liabilities were in front of the room on public display. Bird's eyes quickly scanned the list of assets on the slide. Her salon was up there!

She took in breaths in short sips and briefly shut her eyes. *Father God, Momma, hear my prayer. Talk to me, Jesus. What's going on? Please, God. What did Lem do, putting all of our personal business up here for strangers to see—just for homework!*

Her eyes popped open and she listened to his words so hard that she thought her ears would bleed. He sounded so confident. His information was so tight. Heaven help her, he looked so good. Something primal stirred within her. Her mother's voice registered in the back of her head. *"Be careful what you pray for, Bird, you just might get it."*

A professional, educated, suave and debonair man held the room enthralled. A man who mysteriously looked so much like her husband, a man who she swore she'd known.

"Thank you," he ended with confidence. "Are there any questions?"

Bird sat on her hands. Hell, yeah, there were questions! About two hundred and twenty-five thousand of them! How dare he tell people their marital net worth without asking her first? But he did look good. And sounded even better. She struggled not to smile.

"You say that you have already gotten agreement from the sellers to take back the mortgage on this property, and have given them good faith money to hold it—three thousand last week?" a white man from the important-people section in the front row asked.

"Yes," Lem replied. "With a one-year grace period, and contingencies for the start of financing and the construction completion."

The man nodded and scribbled something down on paper. Lem didn't look at her. His gaze remained fixed on the dignitaries in the front row.

"And I see here that you already have a prospective tenant for the after-school portion of this project," the board president added.

Bird felt her stomach lurch. Was this thing already in process? Did she hear right—her husband had bought a building? When? No. Couldn't be. Okay, okay, okay, they had to play the whole thing through to the bone. Lem was not out of his mind—she had to remember that. Trust the man, don't blow his evening, not when he was doing so well. That's the kind of thing that always started a mess between them. *Just listen, Bird*, she told herself. *Just listen.*

"That's right," Iola Carter cut in, issuing a million-dollar smile at Lem. "And, through our agency list of alumni students, finding tenants with sound businesses and financing already under way will be no problem. We can assist Mr. Van Adams with finding legitimate rental clients. We just wanted to demonstrate the potential—what could be accomplished, if this project ever went forward."

Whew. Bird let out her breath in a sigh of relief. The sister had said *demonstrate,* and *if.* They were talking future tense, not present tense. Okay. Okay. This was a mock presentation. Homework, to dry run what a real transaction would look like. Bird's hand found the center of her chest, and she sat back a bit in her chair.

"It's about creating synergy, Mrs. McFarland," Lem pressed on, addressing the board president. "Each business or tenant would feed and strengthen the other. Let me show you how this concept comes together."

Aw . . . look at her baby. He better work it! Bird began rocking slightly in her chair as her husband turned on some invisible afterburner. He was handling his shit to the max. He had white folks and bourgeois black folks on the edge of their chairs. He was telling them what he believed was possible, and it made too much sense. The brother was on fire.

"You go, boy," she murmured, unable to stop her mouth from forming the words. She hugged herself as Lem spoke, tears threatening her composure. Pride almost made her stand up, but she forced herself to remain seated.

"Each shop by itself, in this transitional neighborhood, would be at risk—if each relied solely on its own foot traffic and marketing. However, as a combined unit, the Shoppes at Van Adams would attract people to the restaurant, which in turn would feed the poetry-comedy venue. The same demographic, we have found based on research, would also likely patronize the full salon and day spa and the boutique, and this culturally aware target market would also support the Afrocentric bookstore. The bookstore's café is also perfect for small gatherings and overflow from the club, while the bookstore can feature local artists—which in turn would feed right back into the club. In addition, these same people have a profile that suggests a boutique is necessary to round out the options. And naturally, the after-school program is not only supportive to the community, but insures a steady stream of young workforce for the shops, as well as consumers—the parents provide consistent foot traffic."

Did her man say full day spa, her dream? Had he actually heard her all these years, and incorporated her fantasy into his own? That he cared so much made Bird bring her fingers to her lips. *He'd heard her.* That's why the salon was up there. God bless him. She was a part of his mock presentation; he'd included her in his vision.

Lem walked away from the new slide he'd just added to the screen and leaned forward on the podium to brace himself. "All the stores get the collective benefit of co-marketing, as well as the overflow from the other businesses within the complex, and they can leverage shared coupons, promotions, and advertising—thereby stabilizing multiple job-creating businesses at once." He paused again as if for dramatic effect, and stood back. "Now, are there any additional questions?"

The long table of board members and instructors whispered to each other, their murmurs indecipherable as they slid pads between them and discreetly conferred with one another.

"The board is satisfied, at this juncture, Mr. Van Adams."

Claire McFarland rose from her seat slowly, and the other members at the table seated with her followed suit. A slow clapping sound began from the row of people in front of Bird, and soon the room thundered with applause. Too short to see over them, Bird shot out of her chair so that she could keep her eyes on her husband. Her gaze tore around the room at the people beside and behind her, who were all on their feet, laughing and whooping. A weird sense of triumph ignited her hands to strike each other repeatedly. The crowd was clapping for Lem—her man was in the midst of a standing ovation!

Instructors had left their chairs and were with him at the front of the room. People she'd just met were pumping Lem's hand. Her vision blurred as she watched his brilliant smile light up his face. Ever since she'd met him, she'd prayed for something like this to happen for him, both for his sake and hers. A thousand thoughts wrestled in her mind at once. The cacophony of voices, cheers, and the ring of clapping hands made her dizzy. Her man had made her proud beyond her wildest imagination.

Her vision blurred again and she dabbed at the corners of her eyes. The lady who looked like Teri was at the microphone, trying to settle the excitement in the room. After several attempts, the ruckus finally died down. Iola Carter's arm was over Lem's shoulder, but her gaze was platonic. Cool. Her man's eyes were on *her*—his wife, where they should have been, and not on the instructor beside him.

Bird gave Lem a huge smile and blew him a kiss. His eyes said "thank you." His lips mouthed, "I love you."

"Well," Iola Carter said with a quick rush. "Now you can see why we had your family members here for twelve long weeks. Now you can see why agencies like ours exist. Now you can see what a little spit and polish can do to a dream—but it took the hard work and sacrifice of the graduates of our class today." She removed her arm from Lem's shoulder, and extended her hand to shake his. "Taking top honors from our class and within our program, Lem Van Adams: presentation award winner of the 2002 graduating class of the Community Development Corporation Center."

Again a thunder of applause surrounded Bird as she watched her husband accept a certificate and a hug from the instructor at the podium. Whoops of support came from each of the graduates' families as the other students took their place alongside Lem. Flashes from cameras went off, and Bird saw wives and husbands, mothers and fathers, old aunties, and friends hugging each other, slapping high fives, wiping away tears of joy. If he'd just told her, she would have had a camera, too! Her baby had been in competition to take best presentation tonight. Now it all made sense, she understood why it had all been made to sound so real. She loved him so much. This was the best surprise, besides Jay, that he'd ever given her!

Bird looked at the students who stood in a row in the front. They had each come into that room seeming edgy, their eyes holding deer-in-the-headlights fear in them—now she knew why. And now they proudly clutched certificates in their hands, triumphant, her husband among them.

Some students wiped at their eyes. Some swallowed hard. Some, like her husband, gave away their emotions only with a pulsing tick of muscle in their jaws. She wondered how many of them had a record. How many of them had ever graduated from anywhere else before this night? How many of them had been cast away and written off by the system, yet had made it this far by faith? And how many people in that line had never been honored before this? How many of those people before her had never been believed in?

The magnitude of what Lem had accomplished made tears trickle down her cheeks. She couldn't wipe them away because her hands were still clapping, bound to the rhythm that was propelled by pride, love, and so much faith. Her hands, hot from friction, slapped together to make a joyful noise. The sound was to transmit dignity . . . resounding accolades for a job well done.

Soon Bird saw the line break and the crowd dispersed, everyone going in different directions to claim their family with open, loving arms. Bird pushed her way through, her short frame barely a match for the larger folks who had more girth. Nothing would keep her from her Lem.

He was wading through the crowd, trying to reach her, too. If only Teri could have been there.... If only Maxine could have seen him, and Kenny could have witnessed his brother-in-law in action. Oh, God, if Jay could have seen his father.

Momma Joe, looking down from Heaven, had to be so proud.

Laughter entered her ear up close, strong arms went around her waist, and her body lifted. Lips met her cheek and then found her mouth. Her husband swung her in a circle, then put her down but didn't let her go.

"I did okay?"

Her hand touched his face as her gaze locked within his. "You did more than okay," she whispered.

"I wanted to surprise you," he murmured, leading her to the buffet tables.

"Oh, you surprised me, all right," Bird said, chuckling.

"But I did good?" He stopped and looked at her, searching her face.

"You did wonderfully," she whispered, pecking his cheek.

"I wanna get out of here, but I need to mingle a bit, thank my instructors and stuff, politics with the board, and then we can go get some real food. Okay, baby?"

"You go do what you've gotta do. I'll munch on some more cheese doodads, and grab a slice of graduation cake. I'll be fine."

He thanked her without words, landing a quick kiss on her forehead before blending into the crowd. She watched him shake hands, receive slaps on his back, and talk in very intellectual tones to the important people. Too bad it wasn't real. All that work to do a mock proposal? It must have been hard, and she felt a twinge of remorse for doubting his whereabouts while he was secretly going to school. But, she reasoned, picking out a juicy strawberry to go with her cheese selection, Lem had learned so much from taking this class that maybe one day Kenny would let Lem co-run Chadway Towing. Too bad Kenny and Maxine weren't here to see it firsthand, as they'd swear she was lying when she told them all about it.

Bird bit into the sweet fruit. Yeah. It was all good.

"Aw, baby," Bird whined. "What are we doing on Forty-third and Calumet, when Pearl's Place is back the other way? I'm hungry and want to get some real, home-cooked-type food."

"I know," Lem said, his gaze going out the window past Bird. "But I wanted to show her to you."

"Show me who?" Bird folded her arms over her chest and sighed hard. She'd had enough meeting and greeting for one night.

"The Van Adams Building."

Her heart almost stopped beating. She had to remember to breathe.

"You mean this wasn't some theoretical—"

"No, she exists," Lem exclaimed. "This is the actual location I based the presentation on. Look at her," he murmured, forcing Bird's gaze to follow his. "This is what she looks like now, but if I'm given the chance to do her right, she'll look like what I showed everybody during the presentation. God, she's gorgeous."

Bird pursed her lips together to keep from speaking. Yeah . . . *if*. It was one thing to dream about it, or do a presentation as a final class assignment—it was another thing to actually do it. But tonight she'd allow him to dream and revel in his accomplishment, wouldn't spoil his natural high. She closed her eyes to help her find a place to begin, and felt the immediate warmth of Lem's hands on either side of her face.

"Oh, baby," he murmured into her mouth.

As she returned his kiss he deepened it, then broke away to land a series of ardent kisses on her forehead, eyelids, and the bridge of her nose before returning to her mouth.

"I love you so much, Bird," he told her in a harsh whisper against her neck. "Have you any idea what I went through to get this far, to keep it all on the down low until I could bring it to you right? But you hung in there with me, and believed in me."

He pulled back. She stared at him. Her husband was breathing hard and the intense gaze that issued from his eyes almost burned a hole in her.

"Never in my life have I felt like this, baby."

What could she say?

"I'm going to do this. I can feel it. They will definitely finance this dream—especially after tonight."

She froze. The brother was losing touch with reality.

Lem's body fell back against his seat and he slapped the dashboard as he did so. "Damn! A brother was on tonight like *hot butter-popcorn!* And my baby was there."

He turned toward her once more, a crazed, impassioned expression on his face.

"Did you see the crowd, Bird? A damned standing ovation; my shit was so *on*. I studied so hard. Every waking minute, I was saying my presentation in my head. Every chance I got, I was dodging to the library, going on the Internet, finding facts and figures, dropping by the Center to run the numbers again—and standing on this corner to see how many people passed by at every conceivable hour of the day and night."

"Oh, Lem . . ." What could she say? How could she say it? There was just so much to consider. So much that she needed to be sure of, before she plunked down the salon as backup for anything he was gonna do. He had to understand that, but right now there was too much voltage in his system to discuss it. *Later,* she told herself, *later.* In the morning he'd be thinking clearer, and she could then say what was on her mind. Not now.

"I knew you'd be there for me," he whispered, his finger tracing the outline of her cheek. "I just knew it."

But her salon? Was he mad?

"I . . ."

For Better, For Worse 115

Bird's words were cut off by her husband's lips upon her own.

"I know, baby," he panted as their kiss broke. "I feel it, too. Wanna just go home? Order Chinese, or pizza, or something? I don't think I can hang at a restaurant, you know?"

His lids had gone heavy, half closed, and his breath was filling her mouth. His face was so near. She'd never seen him like this. But the salon part . . .

"But Jay is at—"

"I'll get Jay when we're done."

When we're done? Oh, yeah. He was over the top now. They needed to talk about a major family decision first. Not just jump between the sheets as if that would make everything all right!

"Bird, let the baby stay with your sister tonight. I'll make us another one tonight. I promise."

His voice was so low, so mellow, and so smooth that the vibration from the deep notes made her belly tremble. He had to cut it out. But, Lord, the way he'd just breathed the words and pulled her earlobe into his mouth when he'd spoken . . . No! Whatever Lem was packing tonight was not prying her salon away from her.

"Baby, we need to—"

"I know," he interrupted with a shiver. "We need to get out of here, don't we?"

His shiver was followed by a slow hiss of air that slipped from his mouth between his teeth. The sound connected to the base of her spine and sent a tremor up the length of it, making her visibly tremble. She squeezed her knees together, and watched him take note of that action. It made him close his eyes. Oh shit, now she'd done it. *They needed to talk.*

Again, strong hands held her face in a tender vise, and then slid down her shoulders. In two minutes he'd be climbing into her seat with her.

"But, but . . . Maxine. I've got to—"

"Call her later, after we're done." Lem's low rumble reverberated inside her chest through her coat. "Just let me take you home. *For real, for real, Bird.*"

"Okay." It was the only way to get him driving the car again, so she could think. Damn. Think, sistah, think!

Lem cut his eyes toward her, his smile sexy. No question about it, when she got home . . . But she needed time to pull her head together. He shifted into drive and peeled away from the curb. She looked at the dilapidated building one more time as they left. *This was going to swallow up her salon whole?* Oh, God. This is what had given her husband a hard-on in the street just now? Double oh, God. This project was what she'd have to explain to her sisters, and her sister's husband—who'd be losing a key employee from Chadway Towing, just as he was getting his big contract under way? Triple oh, my God. It was just supposed to be a demonstration of what could happen—not something real. Homework. A class exercise. That was it.

She monitored the pulse in Lem's jaw by the way the muscle in it tightened and released. Half of her knew that she'd be in for the best rock-the-house evening she'd had in a week, if not in their relationship. The other half of her was working out logistics—family logistics, financial logistics. Lord have mercy! Not the salon.

Her husband practically slammed into a parked car as he swung around the corner and into their driveway. Before she could get off her seat belt and collect her purse, he'd gotten out on his side, rounded the vehicle, flung open the passenger's door, and was kissing her so hard that her hands couldn't find the seat belt button.

"My purse, Lem," she finally gasped, pushing him away.

"Oh, I'm sorry, baby. Here," he said, handing it to her and helping her a little too vigorously out of the car so that she almost bumped her head.

"Damn, boy, slow down." Bird fussed as he ushered her up the steps. Between his pulling her and the wind pushing her, it took everything she had to keep from falling.

His hands literally shook as he fumbled with the front door keys, and finally got the locks to turn. She didn't say a word. This didn't make any kind of sense.

"Look," she said, trying to hold her ground as the door slammed behind her. "We need to—"

"I know, baby." He was on her, cutting off her words, pressing her back against the closed door. "It's just that I love you so much."

Now what was she supposed to say to that mess?

"Take off your coat, at least. Dang," she managed to choke out.

"Right. You're right." He chuckled, but allowed only a sliver of space between their bodies to do so. He threw his good coat, and it missed a chair.

"Let me hang up my coat and take off Teri's pearls before you break 'em, okay?"

Yeah. He could do that. He had to slow down. Chill.

But his wife looked so damned good. She'd had his back. She was there to see him at the best he'd ever been in his life. The only thing that felt close to this moment was when she'd put Jay in his arms. She'd been with him for better or worse, for richer or poorer. Tonight, he'd repay her in full.

Somewhere within his reserves of discipline, he was able to help her off with her coat, and hang it up. It took everything within him to allow her to cross the room a pace ahead of him and begin to take off her jewelry. Closing the gap between them, his hands found her waist, but the wry smile she gave him was his immediate undoing.

He wasn't sure how they fell, not that he cared. The sofa broke what would have been a hard landing if they'd missed it, if he'd miscalculated. But he was on tonight. Hell, yeah.

And beneath him was a warm, breathing woman—his wife. Her gasps filled his ear and disconnected discipline from his brain. He sought her shoulder and the tender side of her neck. She smelled so good . . . and oh, God, she felt so good.

"We have to go upstairs, Lem. Not down here, where family might—"

His mouth stopped her complaint. Legs silken with stockings slid against his palms. Her scent was intoxicating, her dress, so easy to push up and over her hips, her full, high breasts spilled out of the low-scooped neck. When he anointed them with a kiss, though, she moaned, *"Stop."*

Was she insane? Stop? "Bird, I can't . . ." A hard shudder claimed him, and a whimper escaped her mouth. He could feel her fists at his back, clutching his suit jacket.

Then he heard her say, "I love you," and her arms held him tight.

She was there for him, his woman. She held him, his woman. She gave him everything, his woman.

The smell of coffee stirred him, and he slowly rolled over on his back. Every muscle in his body felt like he'd been put on a rack and beaten. Even if Bird was on the Pill, there was no way she wasn't pregnant this morning. Not after last night.

He chuckled to himself and threw a rubbery arm over his forehead. "Oh, God . . ." He couldn't move. He'd lost count of how many times they'd made love. Only the pull of sleep had finally cooled their engines. He chuckled again. Yeah. He was on, last night.

"You think you can make it to work this morning?" She stood in the doorway of their bedroom like a roughed-up angel, holding a cup of coffee and her hair sticking up all over her head.

He laughed a slow, easy laugh of contentment.

"Truth be told, I don't know if I can get up. It's all your fault, woman. You wore a brother out."

"Me?" she scoffed. She brought the mug to the side of the bed for him, and then sat down.

He smelled the brew as she passed it under his nose, the aroma wafting up his nostrils and helping him to come alive. She was so pretty. He touched her lilac robe, rubbing her thigh. Soft, just like Bird.

"I think I need a straw." He chuckled and tried to push himself up on an elbow, but gave up when his arm trembled. The muscles in his lower spine seized, and he fell back without resistance. "Or an ambulance."

"You did this to yourself." Bird giggled. "I told you to cut it out."

"I couldn't help myself." He watched the way her body moved under her silk robe as she talked, the way her breasts shifted under the thin fabric. His gaze traveled down her and rested on her lap. Sweet, heavenly sanctuary, thy name is woman. . . .

"Stop. Don't even go there. I couldn't even get off a call to my sister to see if our son was all right, 'cause you attacked me as soon as we walked in the door."

"Yeah. I did, didn't I?" He chuckled low in his throat and threw his arm back over his eyes to block out the sunlight. "Just a few more minutes, and I'll get up. I feel like a truck hit me last night. Be nice, Bird."

"Well, since my salon had better turn a profit, I guess one of us has to go to work this morning."

He froze. Uh oh. Bullshit was coming. He could feel it like a change in the weather. He was not going to say a mumblin' word; he was in no condition to lock his brain around an argument.

Coffee was the medicine he needed. Lem sat up and took his mug from his wife. "Thanks, baby." That was all he was going to say.

"We need to talk. You know that, right? We have some serious things to discuss."

He nodded and took a slurp of hot coffee. "Yeah, we do," he said, swallowing the brew hard. "We do."

"Then, let's talk."

"I have to go to the bathroom first. Okay? We'll talk. Promise."

He watched her grudgingly move over and accept the mug from him so he could get up. He also took his time with the process of standing, crossing the room, and going down the hall. He needed time—space—to think.

As he stood before the john, his mind latched on to as many facts as it could grasp. What was he going to tell his wife?

When he turned around, he almost jumped out of his skin. Bird was leaning against the bathroom doorframe; her arms were folded over her chest. Women didn't fight fair. They waited until a brother was all jacked up, feeling mellow, too weak to defend himself, and then they beat his ass down with the early-morning logic.

Lem flushed the toilet and washed his hands, splashing cold water on his face, and he held on to the sides of the sink. "Whatever we discuss, and what you saw last night, needs to stay between us, Bird. Let's me and you work this out as man and wife, without an amen section from the family." There, he'd said it.

"And what's that supposed to mean?"

"You know what I mean," he said quietly, but his voice was firm. "Me and you, man and wife, no outside opinions—period. This is too important."

"Okay."

Uh uh. That was too easy.

"Bird, I'm serious," he repeated.

"Why couldn't you tell me what you were up to, then?"

"Because I wanted to be sure that it wasn't just a pipe dream. I didn't want to get people all hyped up and excited, especially you, if I didn't even have a chance."

"Oh." Her voice was calm.

Too calm.

"Then why wouldn't you let me help you?"

She had him trapped in the bathroom. This was no position for a man to be in. But she blocked his exit, as tiny as she was, with arms folded over her chest, her chin thrust up, and her lips pursed in a pout. Was this the same woman who came to his graduation, gave him a standing ovation—cheered, clapped, and cried, and then became his sexy lover all last night?

Words rattled in his brain, but didn't make sense to him when he tried to string them together. "Because, I wanted to do this on my own, do all the research, do the work, find the resources—without having to have my woman do it for me."

"I thought we were partners."

What could he say to that? Damn...

"I thought we had sat up at night, Lem, as man and wife, and talked about my dream to expand the salon—just like you told me how one day you wanted to own a business of your own?"

"We did, baby. Where do you think all this came from? Me and you." She had to understand. The bathroom felt like it was closing in on him. "I didn't just make this stuff up out of the blue. I based it on what we talked about together, what we had dreamed about at the kitchen table together. Me and you."

"Then why didn't we go into it together, taking it from dream to possible reality together? Huh, Lem? Since it's all about me and you? Why did I have to find out about your plans the way I did?"

Okay, okay, he had points to make, too. This morning, she'd hear them!

"Weren't you the one who always said that even though you loved Teri, and were grateful that she supported your business, you never wanted to have to go to her for money, or another family project like that again?"

"Yes, but—"

"Wait, now. Hear me out." Only a small window of opportunity existed as his wife paused, and he rushed in to fill it with words before Bird's mind closed. "And you know how much we've both wanted to do something on our own, without having to always go to the family—"

"But—"

"And, sweetheart, how many times have you told

me that you were sick of them treating you like a baby, and acting like I was no good? That you wanted to one day show them all. Huh?"

When she didn't immediately answer, he folded his arms over his chest. Now they were getting somewhere. He could get her to see. Yeah.

"And couldn't we have done this together, Lem?"

"I wanted to do like you said, honey; take charge of my destiny. Stop whining about the past, as you and Teri always throw in my face—not that I do. I wanted to bring you something on my own, as a man."

"Oh. But you can pledge my salon without asking me, and buy a building with joint household money from our account without consulting me? You don't mind letting me help like *that*. So last night, that presentation was real—that much, you can do all by yourself—as a man, right? And all of these man-made decisions went down without consulting me, your wife. In your wildest dreams, *man*."

"Did I look like I was playin' in front of all those people last night? How did you leave that place thinking it was just a homework exercise?" Bird had to be out of her mind. He wasn't even trying to address the other questions she'd hurled at him—not till he got an answer for them, anyway. "Did it seem like I was playin' *at any time* last night? Especially once we got home?" He pounded on the sink and pushed away from it.

It felt like she'd just driven a stake through the center of his chest . . . right where his pride resided.

He brushed past her and gave himself space. He

needed to get dressed to go to work and get the hell out of there.

"You never consulted me when you decided to open a salon, or to borrow the money to finance it from your sister," he hollered as she entered the bedroom on his heels. "And when you wanted a new car, you never asked me about it first—you just did it."

"That was different." Her voice had escalated a notch.

"Why, Bird? Because you could? Because you had resources—which meant that you had the *power* to do what you wanted, when you wanted?"

The two stared at each other. Only the bed stood between them.

"Have you ever thought about, or asked me, what *I* might want to do—or why I'm doing this?"

She didn't answer.

"Look around, Bird. We're living in your parents' house. Maybe I'd like to take you and Jay on a drive to the realtors. Maybe I'd like to say, 'Baby, pick out what you want in our price range.' Maybe I'd like to go with you to buy furniture that we like, that we can screw on—without worrying about the flowered sofa your momma and daddy had for fifty years. Maybe, just maybe, I'd like to do what you take for granted every day, which is to go into my *own* shop, open it up, and run it. Ever thought about that?"

"So that gives you the right to jeopardize my business, for yours?"

"What happened to 'Baby, we're in this together for better or worse—what's mine is yours and yours is mine?' Huh! And why all of a sudden is my business plan, which experts agree is a sound idea, jeopardizing your salon?"

"You could have told me first, Lem . . ."

The fact that tears stood in her eyes, and that her voice had gone soft, would not move him. No. He was not having it! She'd seen what he could accomplish on his own. She'd seen the way people had believed in him, had cheered for him, and supported him. Her tears and gentleness were a cut-him-to-the-bone weapon; she knew it and was using it.

"Last night, I felt like I was a man. I felt like there wasn't anything I couldn't do. Last night I felt like I had a shot at repaying you for all the years of tears, heartache, and worry. It was as if all the things you told me you wanted, and the things we'd dreamed about together, could actually happen—and I could be the one in the lead for once, who could make those dreams come true for us—for our family! And I felt like my son would one day have a chance to rise above anything out there in the streets. Yet, this morning, I'm defending that? Forget it, Bird. I'm out. I gotta go to work."

He snatched a fresh uniform and some underwear out of the dresser, brushed by Bird, and headed for the shower. "Damn!"

The bathroom door slammed so hard that a paint chip hit the floor. He turned on the shower, jumped in, jumped out when he immediately got scalded, cursed again, then adjusted the temperature knobs until he could ease his way back into the spray.

"I fuckin' work like a mule to keep my end of the marital bargain, do what I'm supposed to do, hand my woman a future on a silver platter that she told me she wanted, and still that shit ain't good enough!" He took out his frustration against his skin with soap and a washcloth in jerky movements.

Abruptly stepping out of the shower, he turned it off, toweled himself dry, and pulled on his clothes. Not today. *Just not today.*

Bird listened to her husband storm out of the house. Finding the edge of the bed, she slowly sat down and closed her eyes as his car pulled away from the space beside the house with an angry screech. She prayed for his safety as he went about his day, and she consulted the only person she could at the moment: God.

On the one hand, Lem was right. It was the most sensible, plausible opportunity in the world. His building contained everything they both loved and had talked about: music, good food, nice shops, dancing, books, nightlife, a bigger salon, and children. It held everything they were good at doing together. It was as if he had taken all their pillow talk and put it down on paper, and had an artist draw it, too.

He'd obviously worked hard to gather the facts, to check and double-check his information, to the point where even experts agreed with him. She'd known for a long time that he wasn't happy living here, though this home felt like a sanctuary to her. And she knew why he didn't tell her until the presentation was a lock. She might have done the same. The man wouldn't have stood a chance if family got into it before he'd found out for himself what he was capable of.

She folded her arms about herself at her waist and squeezed her closed eyes more tightly. This was bad. Really, really bad. This was about a man's self worth—a vulnerable place where no woman should ever go.

Yet there had been so many disappointments, so many dramas between them. The salon was her protection against the world. If Lem ever got incarcerated again or did something shaky, Cut It Up was the only thing she had to take care of her and her son. This project of his would suck up all their assets: cash in the bank, the salon, and possibly her portion of her parents' home. Rather than a pipe dream, the salon was something tangible. The choice landed her between a rock and a hard place: give up her husband, or give up a secure future for her son.

Bird wiped at the silent tears streaming down her face. Her sisters could not get in it at this juncture. Teri would flip, and then she'd just lose her husband to a hypothetical argument. Anyone with common sense knew that things could go wrong with the financing at the last minute, and then maybe she'd be off the hook. So why kick up dust now? There were so many variables. *Patience,* Bird told herself. *Patience.* Maxine would probably approve, but it might put a permanent rift between Lem and Kenny. Lem didn't need to break the only solid, honorable male bond he had. Not for a dream.

Bird stood and faced the sunshine. Her gaze went through the window to the changing colors of the falling leaves. The wind whipped them around, creating swirls of hue on the dying amber grass. She should have listened to her mother. If she didn't have anything good to say, she shouldn't have said anything at all. Not today. Not after last night. Not so soon. If only she'd had the wisdom to wait just one more day. . . .

But right now, she had to go get her son.

six

bird knew mornings were a bad time to try to talk to Maxine. Her sister's household looked like a Chicago Transportation Authority depot then. Maxine would be shooing Ahmad out the door to catch his school bus, arguing with Kelly to get her coat on and to leave her doll babies alone, and the baby might be wailing for attention. If Kenny were there, he'd be late, grumpy, and hollering to her sister to find this or that. Jay would be in the midst of the chaos, probably giving Maxine the blues about not wanting to be in a high chair, or not wanting to eat his cereal. What she needed to discuss was not something you dropped on a sister at rush hour.

She rang the bell and waited. She could hear the commotion behind the door as Maxine's loud calls for order rose above the din. Her sister looked frazzled when she opened the door, and Maxine kissed her quickly on the cheek.

"Hey, baby," Maxine said in a hurried tone, not even staying put long enough for Bird to return her kiss. "Ahmad," she called up the stairs. "If I have to tell you again, and if I have to come up there, boy!"

"All right, Mom!"

"Who do you think you talkin' to like that, Ahmad?" Maxine stood at the bottom of the staircase with her baby daughter on her hip. "You'd better get an attitude adjustment when you answer me, boy—and get it quick!" Then Maxine headed for the kitchen, stopping to turn off Kelly's cartoons on TV despite the child's protests, as she moved through the house like a runaway train.

Bird greeted her dejected niece and followed Maxine. "Thanks for watching Jay last night," she offered, going toward her sticky son, who was banging a spoon on the high chair tray.

"No problem," Maxine replied, pulling lunches out of the fridge. "As usual, he was an angel."

Jay greeted Bird with a squeal of recognition and reached for her. His happy, upturned face was what she needed this morning. She scooped him up with joy and hugged him hard. "Mommy missed you," she whispered against the soft, cereal-plastered cheek that nestled next to hers.

"His diaper bag is by the door, with his coat and hat," Maxine told her. "You taking him to the regular baby-sitter, Mrs. Jenkins, for the day?"

"Yeah." Bird put the discarded spoon and bowl from the high chair into the sink with the rest of the dishes.

"Oh, girl, just leave that," Maxine fussed. "I'll deal with that when I get back from the morning runs. I've gotta get Kelly to school, and this little bird into a coat." Maxine left the refrigerator, clutching a handful of lunches. "Ahmad!"

How did her sister keep it all together? Kenny was a good man, but no saint. Yet somehow, Maxine seemed to keep an efficient handle on things in a crazy-busy household.

"You need me to watch him tonight, or something?"

"No," Bird said in a quiet voice. "I'll pick him up from Mrs. Jenkins on my way home—since I don't know what time Lem will be back tonight."

"Yeah, I hear you," Maxine grumbled, tugging on her daughter's coat and hat as the infant desperately wriggled to disallow her mother to do so. "Never know what time they'll be in with this new tow contract, not that I'm complaining, Father God. Thank you for the abundance this family needs. Amen." Maxine sighed as the prayer-comment left her mouth. "But *I'm always here.*" She glanced at Bird, then back at her fidgeting daughter in her lap. "So, hey, one more won't hurt."

There was something in Maxine's tone that made Bird pause, but now wasn't the time to address it. They could talk later. Right now, she had to transfer Jay to the next pair of loving arms that would hold him, and then go open her shop for the sisters that came in before they had to go to work. The newly extended hours of her shop brought in fat revenues; she had to be there.

Bird made her way to Maxine through the clamoring children, kissed her nieces and her nephew, and then her sister. It was like trying to jump into a double-Dutch rope. You had to weave and bob until there was a split-second opening, have perfect timing to get in and get your turn, keep up the pace—then skillfully get out.

"Bye," Maxine called behind her. "Have a nice day!"

Bird drove around the corner and pulled up to Mrs. Jenkins's house. After struggling to get Jay out of his car seat in his bundled-up, snowsuit condition, she handed her son over to the gentle older woman who reminded her so much of her mother. God, she missed her mom. Jay went right to Mrs. Jenkins without a fuss, and this morning she was glad that her son hadn't clung to her, demanding that she not leave him. On the other hand, a part of her ached that her baby could so easily go to someone else's arms.

Bird shook the eerie feeling. It reminded her too much of Lem. Maybe, one day, he'd go to someone else who spoiled him like Mrs. Jenkins spoiled Jay. There might be some sister our there who'd give him anything he wanted, whether it was good for him or not. Maybe someone pretty, like Iola Carter. . . . No, she told herself. She was *not* going to go there.

She didn't even turn on the radio when she got back into her car; she needed pure silence. She needed to think.

"Chill," she told herself out loud when she reached the salon.

Her shop.

Pretty salmon-colored walls greeted her as she flipped on the lights and walked in. Locking the door behind her, she kept the Closed sign facing the street to give her the half hour she needed to set up for the day. This was her domain, where she made all decisions. She hired, fired, and developed all the promotion ideas. She handled the money. Here, she was queen. And her husband wanted her to give this up?

Bird's stomach gurgled, and the churning coffee in her belly made her slightly nauseous as she entered her small back office. Picking up messages, she looked at the appointment book. Good. She had forty-five minutes before a perm walked in.

She sat down heavily in her deep pink, custom leather swivel chair, and reached into the drawer for a pack of cheese-and-peanut-butter crackers. Years at the salon had taught her to keep some food stashed, because when it got busy, there was no telling when a sister could take five, get off her feet, and grab a bite. But the crackers tasted a little off. Everything on her tongue felt coated by a bitter taste. She hurled the half-bitten cracker into her waste can, making a mental note to dump it at the end of the day, lest six-legged friends start to visit the salon. No one was allowed to leave open food in her shop anywhere, not even in the trash. Roaches in her salon? Hell, no!

If Lem had any sense of responsibility, he'd understand what it was like to have your own and not want to put it at risk.

Bird closed her eyes and allowed her body to relax

against the soft, buttery feel of the leather. All she needed to do was calm down. He'd come around and understand. He didn't have a choice.

However, as she sat still, taking in the quiet before she turned on the radio to infuse high-energy music through the shop, nagging questions jumped into her mind.

On the one hand, Lem had a point. If they were husband and wife, then everything they had should be a joint venture—especially if it made sense. Were the shoe on the other foot, and if Lem had a towing business or something, and if her dream was to open a salon—how would she feel if he told her that his business was off-limits? The question brought more acid to her tongue and she went to the water cooler and tried to swallow down the nasty taste.

Her mind latched on to the morning scene at Maxine's house. What if that were her? What if her husband had a great business, but didn't recognize what she wanted to do? "He who has all the gold makes all the rules," she quoted into the empty space, downing more water and tossing the paper cup into the trash. She needed a mint, a piece of hard candy, or something.

Searching for the candy stash in the cabinet beneath her desk, she unscrewed the tight lid from the shop's jar of colorful, individually wrapped candies. She picked out a cherry-flavored one and popped it into her mouth, then sat back down. She wasn't being totally fair to Lem. She wouldn't want to live in his mother's house—even if the woman passed away.

She'd be champing at the bit to get out of there. Okay. He had a point there, too.

However, she didn't have a shaky track record like he did. It was plain stupid for a woman to put everything on the table for love. Uh, uh. God bless the child who had her own.

Look at what happened to Teri; educated, brilliant, and an attorney. That didn't stop two ex-husbands from cleaning her clock financially! But Teri still had something to fall back on after all the drama.

Bird stood. It was time to drop this mental debate, which could go on for hours. She had to get the salon ready for clients. The salon was a real, viable, functioning business; a legacy for her son, and not a dream. She was willing to forgive Lem's past, but wasn't sure she could ever forget it. Any sister in her right mind could never forget, even if she could forgive. She'd been burned by his irresponsibility before.

Lem stood in front of the building, allowing the icy winds to slap his face with reality. He could barely breathe as grief and the cold stole the air from his lungs while he stared up at it, saying good-bye to his dream. "We made it this far, baby," he said sadly, leaning against the tow truck. "We made it this far. It was good while it lasted, but it's over."

Dropping this on his coaches was going to be hard, too. He envisioned the stricken look on Iola Carter's face, then wondered how Russell Hampton or Linda Maxwell would take it. Each one of them had hung in there with him as if they'd have taken a bullet for him—and professionally, they had.

Lem shook his head with disgust and turned his back on his beloved. He hopped into the truck, pulled out into the street and reached for the radio, blasting DMX. The sound of bass notes rocked his vehicle and competed for space in his mind. Hip-hop rhythms collided with the dispatch radio chatter. He needed noise; anything to block out the pain. He had to take this shit like a man. Wasn't nuthin' new under the sun. A brother knew that.

No woman, not even a wife, was going to do some *Cosby Show*, supportive-husband-and-wife-type shit. He'd been trippin' for twelve weeks. For better or for worse, for richer or poorer, in sickness and in health. Lem chuckled bitterly. Yeah, right. That applied only to the man.

They needed to be honest when they said that shit in church. They needed to say, "Brother, you have to be richer. You cannot be poorer. If you are, then she might let you lodge there, get some, only 'cause she needs some. She might take care of your ass if you get the flu or somethin' light, and might even take you back if you get locked up—but don't try to get into her pocket, boss." Yeah. They needed to be real with the vows. Women never forgot or forgave if you messed up. And honesty was a joke.

A tow call came over the truck radio, and Lem responded, yelling over the ear-splitting music. "Yeah, I got it." Yeah. This time he totally got it.

* * *

"What're you doing?" Bird asked as her sister Teri picked up her cell phone.

"Getting ready for a case, Bird. What am I always doing?"

A soft laugh followed, but Bird could tell her sister was multitasking as they talked.

"Right." Bird chuckled nervously. "Got a minute for your sister?"

There was a pause.

"Is it urgent—a 911, or just a general discussion?"

Again, there was a pause.

"No, it's not urgent," Bird lied. "Just missed your voice."

"Then why did you call me on my cell?"

Bird looked at the clock, and sighed. "Because I figured you'd be in the street at eight P.M., or still at the office."

"Well, if I was in the street, I'd be with a client. If I was in the office, I'd be working—and you could have called on my direct line to it. If I was home, I would have answered. If I wasn't home and you got my machine, and if this wasn't a 911, then you would have left me a message. What's up?"

"Okay, counselor." Bird sat down slowly on a kitchen chair. "Just wanted to eat dinner with you while we chitchatted." Bird picked at her plate, then pushed it away.

"Where is Lem?"

The annoyed tone in Teri's voice made Bird let out a long breath again.

"I don't know."

"Is he still *volunteering?*"

"No," Bird hedged. "That's done. The twelve-week program is over, and doesn't start again for another six weeks."

"Okay, then where is his trifling butt?"

Teri's question was crisp, curt. When she was working, she didn't go into long lectures or speeches—just sound bites. Bird wasn't sure which was worse.

"Look, you're busy, and I was just lonely. Little Jay went down for the night, so I thought I'd just run my mouth with you until Lem got in. He'll be in shortly. Probably working OT for Kenny."

"Have you called the garage?"

Bird hesitated. The last thing she wanted to do was call the garage, and add fuel to the fire by having Lem think she was checking up on him again.

"No."

"Why not?"

"Because I trust him. I just miss him."

"Okay, then, you two lovebirds work it out."

"Yeah, you're right," Bird said, despite the way she was feeling.

"Are you sure you're all right?"

"Yeah. I'm really fine, Teri. Like I said."

"Okay, then. Call Maxine. She could probably use some adult conversation after spending all day with little people. I'm trying to get this brief finished. I'll talk to you tomorrow."

"Okay. Talk to you later."

"Love you. Bye," Teri said quickly, and hung up.

Bird stared at the dead receiver and tapped the Off button on her cordless phone, then hit speed dial for Maxine's number.

"What're you doing?"

Maxine laughed as Bird's voice filled her receiver. "Oh, just settling world peace at my dining room table, trying to help my son learn the history of the Spanish Inquisition, hollering at Kelly to get out of the tub, getting the baby ready to go down for the night, and making Kenny's plate."

"I guess you're busy, then?"

Maxine chuckled. "In a word, yes. But never too busy for you, hon. What's up? Ooops, but hold on a second and let me turn off this pan."

"Okay."

Bird held the phone. Kenny was home, and she could hear his good-natured voice booming in the background as her sister yelled a friendly greeting to him. That meant the garage was either closed, or he was just there for a dinner break. Too many thoughts crowded into her mind in the silence as background noise from the Chadway household went on without interruption. It was like being on a party line as a passive listener. Where was *her* husband?

As she waited for Maxine, she heard a car pulling up into the driveway. Lem was home, and she had to get off the telephone. She stood.

"Hey, Max," she said loudly to get her sister's attention. "Lem is home, I'll call you later."

"Okay, bye, honey," Maxine said briskly. "Sorry it was so crazy when you called—feeding time at the corral. Call me after it slows down a little at your ranch, all right?"

"Yeah, I will," Bird promised. "Love you. Bye."

She held her breath and listened for Lem's homecoming routine to begin. The front door opened. She sat down. Good. At least he'd come home, and they wouldn't have to play that cat-and-mouse game of I'm-angry-at-you-so-I'm-staying-out-late.

Food for him was still on the stove. She heard him hang up his jacket and walk across the living room, then through the dining room. When he came into the kitchen, he didn't speak. *Oh, it was on now.*

"Hello to you, too."

"Hey," he grumbled, opening the refrigerator.

"I made dinner."

"I already ate."

"You could have called so I could put the food away."

He didn't answer. "How's Jay?" he asked instead.

"Fine, and asleep at this hour."

"I'm not in the mood, Bird."

She watched her husband grab a beer and twist off the top. To hell with him and his attitude. "We need to talk."

"About what?" He looked at her hard and took a swig from his beer. "Thought you said all you had to say this morning. I know I did."

"See, that's the problem with you," she bristled. Bird stood and walked over to the stove, and then began snatching down Tupperware from the cabinet to put away leftovers.

"I know," he muttered. "I'm the one who always has the problem. Fine, Bird. I'm going to take a shower."

"You need to stop being so salty and talk to me, not take a damned shower."

He just stared at her.

"The other day, you were sweatin' me because I didn't take a shower. Tonight, I'm wrong because I worked a fourteen-hour shift in the ass-biting cold, am dirty as hell, and want to wash the road sludge off of me."

"This is different," she shot back, slamming the Tupperware she held down onto the sink counter.

He let his breath out hard and then took another swig from his beer bottle. "It's *always* different with you, Bird. Always."

Tears of frustration rose. "Why can't we just talk like normal people? Why does it always have to be some test of wills with you, huh? Why can't we just be honest with each other and talk calmly?"

Lem leaned against the doorframe and cast his gaze out the kitchen window. "Because," he said after a moment, "you don't want me to be honest with you."

"What's *that* supposed to mean?"

Tense silence stood between them like a referee.

"I'm never sure how to put things right, so that it won't start an argument. And truth be told, right now, I'm not in the frame of mind to argue."

She let her breath out hard and plopped down into a chair. Truth be told, she didn't have the energy at the moment to argue, either. "Can't we just sit down at the table and talk like rational people?"

He looked at her with suspicion. "Aw'right. Since I know there'll be no peace until I do," he said in a sullen tone, snatching out a chair and turning it backward to straddle it. "Shoot."

"You want me to trust you, Lem. Right?"

He just continued to glower at her.

"Then, how am I supposed to do that when every time I turn around, you've cooked something up without letting me or anybody else know, and then we wind up cleaning up behind it?"

She watched her husband's expression cloud over even more, and the muscle in his jaw twitch.

Lem took in a deep breath and let it out slowly. "I have tried to talk to you, and everybody in this family, on occasion. But the things I used to do keep getting thrown up in my face. It's like y'all never give that shit a rest."

"That's not fair, Lem, and you know it."

"All right," he said, pushing back from his chair and standing again. "Take any incident that has come between us in recent history. You always say you forgive me, but you never forget a single transgression. Can you tell me I'm lying, and tell me it always doesn't get brought up again after it's supposed to be dead and buried? Name one, Bird."

Oh, now he was going to the bone. "That's *really* not fair," she shot back. His hurtful reminder of arguments past was like peeling back a never-healed scab on a still-tender wound. Who the hell did he think he was talking to!

"Hear me out," he replied, his tone even and controlled. "I love you, Bird. I was about to lose my mind when you were in that car accident. Then you came home, all messed up . . . and I was there, every minute of that."

"I know," she whispered. Why did he have to say that? Damn.

"I didn't cheat. I didn't go looking at other women. I just couldn't process what had happened to my wife. But nobody gave a shit about the effect of all this coming down on my head. The salon was backed up; your ability to function was impaired. Money in the house was jacked. My best friend, Kenny, was all messed up. My son's mother—you—almost died. I was holding a lot in." Lem began walking in a circle and using his hands to speak as his words poured out.

"So, yeah, maybe your husband had a moment there when he didn't feel real amorous temporarily. Or maybe it wasn't even that," he said more quietly. "Maybe your man was thinking, damn, my baby is all messed up and I can't even handle the finances without her salon. That don't exactly give a man wood, you follow me? But I didn't say a word about a thing, wasn't looking for no excuse to why I wasn't feelin' in the mood right then, because I knew it would hurt you—would cut to the bone."

"It did," she whispered, looking away.

"But did I stop loving you, caring for you? No. I needed to adjust to the new situation happening between us. But you pressed, and pressed, and kept asking me what was wrong, and finally I told you—as much as I could figure out in my own head at the time. My bad. I should have *never* said a word about something I wasn't totally sure about. Instead, I should have lied, said I was having prison flashbacks, told you *any* shit but the truth."

"That's not true . . ." her voice trailed off as she swallowed away sudden tears.

"Yes. You think about it, Bird."

His voice had grown stronger, more confident, and carried the tone of righteous indignation. It was as though he were standing there having an epiphany before her eyes. She didn't like it. He was making too much sense, and she was on the wrong side of the new equation.

"My personal business," Lem stated flatly. *"Our* personal business, to be more accurate, was thrown in my face. You went out on the town with this I-didn't-die-so-I'm-embracing-life-'cause-my-screwed-up-husband-doesn't-do-me-right crusade. I had to watch my wife party-hop, tell me what I didn't do for her, a whole buncha nonsense—all because I told the truth."

"Now wait—"

"No, Bird. *You* wait. You flip the script. Suppose I was in an accident. Suppose you had nursed me back to health, been there for me, and everything. And then I got better, but had some equipment problems. Then, if I had brothers, say I went to all of them and told them that my wife had gone dry on me, couldn't give me none."

Bird looked away. Shame burned her face.

"Then," Lem pressed, "say I got a wild hair up my ass because of that, and decided to just say screw it, and started partying—leaving my wife and child home, or buying new cars, doing what I wanted to do without thinking about anybody else? What would the Joseph sisters say?"

Bird shrugged and kept her gaze away from his, knowing the answer too well. She began toying with a saltshaker on the table.

"They'd say, 'Put that sorry, low-life, no-good, no-'count nigger's ass out!'" Lem's breath came in bursts of fury. "They'd say, 'That bastard ain't actin' right, and he should be thanking his Jesus that he's alive and has a good family all intact.' They'd be hollering, 'How could he treat our loyal sister that way after she nursed his sorry behind back to health! Kick his black butt. Go beat him down.' They'd send Kenny after me. Am I right, Bird?"

When she didn't answer, Lem went on. "See, it's two sets of rules, Bird. One for a man; one for a woman. I got clear on that a long time ago. So all this discussion about 'let's talk' is rhetoric. You all can talk; we have to listen. Period.

"I got that. I was out of place, outta line. I messed with the cosmic order of things in the Joseph universe. You all get to dream and dabble in those dreams; women do. We men get to bring home the bling bling—unless we go into the situation already hooked up."

"That's really not fair, Lem." She had to stand her ground. This conversation was not going like it was supposed to. "I bring home the money, too."

"Right!" He laughed. "That's my point."

His laughter sent a chill down her spine as she stared at her husband.

"You just don't get it, do you, Bird?" Lem snatched his beer off the table, turned the bottle up to his lips, then began walking in a tight circle. "Baby brings home the bacon—has from the moment I met her. Now, here's the thing, the double standard. You following me?"

"Go ahead," she said, her gaze locked within his.

"I," he said, slapping the center of his chest, "was incarcerated. Maybe I knew that I needed to get my thing right before I got married. But being realistic, I was also trapped into a situation."

"Oh, so now I trapped you into marrying me?" Bird pushed back in her chair and folded her arms over her chest.

"No," he said calmly. "Not at all. I had the choice of waiting to get my thing right, which could take years, and risk losing you—a sister who made it perfectly clear that her biological clock was ticking, that she wasn't hanging around to get played, and was the marrying kind. Or I could go along with the program—because I couldn't deal with losing you. Time was not on my side, so I needed to get married without my money being straight and then try my best to get my head above water. It's like playing constant catch-up, but I was willing to take that risk, because I loved you so much, Bird. I couldn't stand to think of my woman running off with another brother who had more going for him at that time."

What could she say to that? Shit.

"I love you, too, Lem. It's just that—"

"It's just that, a sister ain't trying to mix the finance with the romance. A sister ain't tryin' to get played by a possibly shaky brother. A sister will have his son, live with him as man and wife, and let him move into her mother's house—but she ain't tryin' to go there with her snaps. Right? I know you love me, baby, but you just don't trust me. What part of this am I not understanding? I'm a basic kinda brother—you can spell it out plain, and I'm cool."

"Lem, it's not like that." Words were failing her. Tears in her eyes were making it hard to see his face clearly. Her man was standing there in the middle of the kitchen floor, dissecting her heart. Yet he was bleeding internally from a mortal wound—she could hear it in his voice.

"It *is* like that," he sighed. "You'll eventually tell your sisters about my little dream, and they'll all laugh about it, and then advise you to steer clear of another of Lem Van Adams's schemes. You all will sit around somebody's table, high-five about how I came in juiced like a fool on my graduation night and rocked your ever-livin' world, but dick or no dick, you wasn't givin' up no salon . . . the brother was trippin'. Then your attorney sister will draw up some formalized agreement to protect all of your assets from the shaky son of a bitch you married, while your other sister goes along with the group."

Lem walked toward the door. "I may not have a degree, but I'm a quick study of human behavior. Been around y'all long enough to know what's up. Got to, to survive."

For Better, For Worse   149

She was out of her chair like a shot to follow him as he left the kitchen and went for his jacket.

"We don't sit around and discuss you like that—I won't tell them about your graduation." Her words sounded false even to her own ears.

He hesitated and just looked at her for a moment, then pulled on his coat slowly, flipping his cap on.

"I wish I had come right, Bird." His voice was so soft that she had to strain to hear it. "I wish I wasn't born down the way, and had gone to school, and stayed out of trouble. I wish I had gotten an education through school, instead of the streets. I wish that when I'd met you, I was starting my own business, and that we could have begun in a little starter apartment, and then built something together. To move into our own house, putting our scrimped-up savings together, and then had Jay, as my business got stronger and you got your own salon. But that's a fantasy. Reality is, I'm out of sequence, baby. Out of order." His gaze went toward the door as he swallowed hard. "I wish a lot of things," he added with a whisper. "*Those* are the things you should ask me about. Not where I been if I'm an hour late—like you're my parole officer. I did my time already."

"Don't go, Lem, not like this."

"Like what, Bird?" He turned now to look at her hard. "I can't go get some fresh air? Is it after lockdown hours in the joint? Just answer me this: have I ever, as long as we been married, been with another woman?"

"No," she said fast, trying to reassure him of her

trust, even though she wasn't sure of it herself. Anything to get him to stay, to keep him talking to her.

"But every time I walk out the door, you sweat me like I was going to one. Ooops, that's right . . . I did take Kenny to a strip joint *one time,* to get that brother's pulse back after he'd been laid up in the hospital. I have a *past* bad record. Yup. Guilty forever."

"It's not the women in the streets I'm worried about."

"See, I keep forgetting. It's my other past. Drug dealing. Hmmm . . . Let me see." Lem dug into his pocket for his keys. "That's right. When I couldn't find a job and the bills were crazy, and my family was on my neck, and I kept getting fired because nobody would let the past die, regardless of how good a job I was doing . . . yeah, I stepped off the straight and narrow, and we separated because I did a deal with my cousin—*one more time*. And even though I never went back to that, worked for your family's grocery store without a hint of doing anything shady, worked for my brother-in-law as the best man on his squad, and bring home my check like clockwork—that *one time* is still kickin' my ass." Lem zipped up his jacket.

Bird opened her mouth, but no words came out.

"I know. There's nothing to say."

His eyes held a level of hurt that she could not fathom. It made her chest feel like something invisible was pressing on it, and the sudden heaviness drew her hand to cover her heart. In the back of her mind she saw flashes of that man who stood before a room and held it hostage with sheer intelligence and force of will, and now she was staring at a man in a dirty baseball cap and filthy tow company jacket, who seemed as though his spirit had just been severed. And worst of all, she felt like she'd held the knife—the blade had been her tongue.

"I know you don't want to get caught up in that risk-factor thing, Bird. Married or not. Don't want to trust me with any joint household finances or endeavors, just in case the one time that you do is the wrong time. Especially since I didn't bring nothing to the table but dick. If that's all you wanted from me, baby, you didn't have to marry me to get it. I'da given you that—and woulda even gave Jay my last name, if that was important to you. See, I learn fast—just ask my coaches from the Center. I was the top of my class for catching on to new shit quick."

"Lem, wait," she whispered, touching his arm.

But he shrugged off her hand, and was out the door.

seven

adrenaline rose with the music, fueled by the bass. "Yeah . . . just rock!" Lem felt the insistent beat through his chest, through his hands that clutched the steering wheel, and up his forearms. "Just rock!" His head kept the rhythm as his car sped down familiar streets—old streets he knew like the back of his hand, just like he knew this song. Street scenes passed like blurs, but he had X-ray vision. The huddles of men talking were businessmen doing transactions. The women walking slowly were night trading. It was all about one's perspective.

The underground economy was alive and well in the streets of Chicago, which might as well have been LA, Philly, New York, or wherever. The story was the same, so was the game. "Let's rock!"

In some neighborhoods, you didn't worry about a ticket or where to park. This was one of them. Five-O had better things to do than to risk their lives holding a pad to ticket a car. The gangs kept them busy enough. Most license plates and tags were bogus anyway. What was the point? It was all a matter of perspective—priority.

Lem walked to the beat that had been in his bones, and his stride became a stroll, a way of walking that he remembered. Cold air became his ally; it numbed his senses. Brothers sized him up, but only nodded as he passed. *Yeah, respect.* Muthas better recognize—he was a brother on the edge. They knew the deal. It was in the eyes. *His* eyes. They had perspective.

His old watering hole was still there, like a beacon in the night. This was sanctuary, and the half-burned-out neon light was a welcoming sign. Nobody would slide away from him in there, or clutch their pocketbooks tight to their sides as he entered. There'd be no hostess to seat you or take your order. Everybody was packin', men and women alike, and everybody knew it—so people were cool. Didn't nobody step on nobody's toes in a joint like this. It was real. He liked it like that. Everybody around the way had perspective.

A blast of heat bombarded him with the deep vibration of bass-line when he opened the door. Oh, yeah . . . let's rock.

"Yo, stranger," the barmaid called from the far end of the bar as Lem made his way to a position with his back toward the wall.

A brother couldn't be too careful. Having one's back against the wall was a state of affairs he'd grown familiar with. He eased onto a stool.

"Hey, Vivian. Long time no see."

"You look good. Whatchu havin'?"

"A brew—what's on tap?"

"A brew?" She pushed her shiny weave curl back from her face with a long orange talon and cocked her head to the side. "C'mon, player—tell me we ain't seen you in all dis time, and you going for the light stuff? How 'bout the usual? A Hennessey for my brother?"

Lem chuckled. "That'll work, Miss Viv. I could use somethin' to knock my head back."

"I can handle that for you, but you have to wait till I get off, lover."

They both laughed. Vivian knew he didn't do old clients.

She brought him his drink and set it down in front of him, leaning forward on the bar so he could see her double-D boobs nearly fall out of her lime-green halter top. "This one's on the house, for an OG that used to open my nose when he walked by." She dipped a talon into his liquor and let the dark liquid drip between her ebony breasts, then sucked the remaining liquor off her finger and smiled.

"Thanks, baby," Lem said with a slow grin. He took a swallow and allowed the taste to slide over his tongue and down his throat with a wince.

"Been a long time, hasn't it?"

"Yeah," he admitted.

"But you still a Boy Scout," she said with a rueful chuckle. "I can tell." Then she winked, and moved down the bar to wait on other customers.

He sat there considering the amber fluid in his glass. He wasn't quite sure why Vivian's dead-on observation disturbed him, but it did. For a moment, he'd almost

For Better, For Worse

felt apologetic that he didn't have any product for her. Visiting grave sites as a ghost had a way of making a man think about his past life, remembering only the good parts of it—the power parts.

Lem took another deep swig, allowing his gaze to evenly rove the room without settling anywhere specific. Here, you kept it sweeping, like you were looking for something, and not singling anyone out in particular—that could get you beat down, or shot. But everybody was scanning the terrain all the time. That was about survival, keeping sharp, not missing anything out of order. That was cool.

His gaze found a familiar pair of eyes as one of his old buddies entered the bar. Lem nodded and let a lazy smile occupy one half of his face. He jumped down from the high, black plastic upholstered stool as his homeboy approached. Both men laughed and a fast embrace followed. His boy was wearing all leather, with a heavy-hittin' Rolex. The diamond studs in both ears were blinding—pure rock. Zip must be doing all right for himself.

"Yo, Dawg . . . damn! Where you been at?" Zip took an open seat beside Lem.

"Been chillin', man." Lem took a final swig from his glass, polishing off what was left in it, and pushed it toward the inside of the bar for Vivian to come get it.

"Now, see," Vivian said as she came to refill Lem's glass and take Zip's order, "the old posse is in the house. What are you havin', Zip?"

"Please," Zip replied. "Don't act like you don't know."

"You're paying for your cognac. You know that level of first drink ain't on the house, not even for OGs," she warned.

The fact that Vivian had given Lem a first free wasn't lost on him, and she winked at him as Zip started to argue.

"You wouldn't give an original gangsta, an OG, a first free?" Zip opened his arms wide and cocked his head to the side, and then shook his head. "You're cold, woman. Cold."

"No. Cold is outside. I'm being real." Vivian laughed and pushed Zip away from her when he tried to lean over the bar to give her a kiss.

"I got you, brother. First round." Lem chuckled, knowing this was why he'd come here. Somehow the drama was oddly relaxing, took a man's mind off the immediate bullshit in his life.

"Well, thank you, *my brother*," Zip said with sarcasm aimed at Vivian. "That's all right, Sis. Forget you, then. My brother's got my back. Next round I'll have his, and so forth. You *can* keep all that tabbed, right? You kin keep our mathematics straight?"

Vivian waved her hand at Zip to dismiss his comment and left them to make their drinks.

"So," Zip inquired, "whassup?"

"Nuthin', man. Just got off work, tired, needed a drink . . . came by the old spot. How you hangin'?"

"I'm cool," Zip told him, accepting the drink from Vivian and tipping his glass in Lem's direction.

Lem followed suit.

"Been investin,' " Zip said.

Lem looked at Zip from the corner of his eye as he leaned on the bar with both elbows, studying the drink in his hand. "That's cool." Zip had dismissed Vivian from their conversation by turning his body sideways to face Lem.

"I'm serious," Zip went on, once Vivian got the message and slipped away to wait on other patrons. "Had my sister hold on to some snaps for me when I hit a bump in the road. When I got out, I dropped it on a coupla laundramats. Was able to parlay that into a corner store, a barbershop, and a check-cashing joint. It's all good."

Tonight, he did not want to hear this shit, even though he was impressed. "How'd you get around the obvious?" Lem asked, despite his better judgment. "That had to be one helluva knot you put up for safekeeping. Money to that magnitude gets tracked."

"True dat," Zip said, taking a careful swallow from his glass. "But if a man has the right connections, he can do a lil' somethin'."

"Word." Lem's thoughts consumed him as both men fell momentarily silent.

"Look, man," Zip finally said. "You and I both know a job ain't you. Damn, bro, look at you—wearing a uniform and shit. This messes me up, seeing you come out and settle for this. What's up?"

"I've turned my life around," Lem said into his glass. A sullen vibration claimed him. He did not come here for this. "Got a family, a wife, a son. Can't go back to the old way, you feel me?"

"I'm not going back to the old way neither, man.

Ain't talking crazy," Zip protested. "You and I both know that half of the so-called legit businesses got started with fast money. But they was smart. They got out—and stayed out. They took bootleg liquor and turned it into presidencies. Or ran prostitutes and numbers, and now they have casinos and hotels and shit. It's a double standard, brother."

"I'm familiar with the double standard aspects of life. And I know all the political rhetoric that goes with it. But I ain't no white boy. I can't rip off people's pensions and make a billion dollars, and sit in front of the cameras with tears in my eyes talkin' 'bout, 'I'm sorry, I didn't know.' Be realistic, Zip. That's the kind of talk we had on the yard—brothers always talking about the unfairness of it all, and planning the next score."

"I'm not talking about a score. I'm talking about investors who need a cool place to put their hot capital. That's why Zip can pick up your tab, and why Miss Vivian ain't offering me no first drinks on the house." Zip motioned out the window with his chin. "Look out there," he said casually. "That's from my check-cashing businesses."

The shiny black Mercedes that was parked on the sidewalk put a bitter taste in Lem's mouth. He took a slow, calm sip from his glass and set it down carefully on the bar, not looking at Zip as he did so. All of a sudden his free drink tasted like charity, instead of respect from his old hangout.

"All legit," Zip urged. "I had enough to get the first laundramat and the building it was in, from my past life piggy bank. Then I got a hookup . . . an old client of yours and mine, an attorney. Remember him?"

Lem nodded, but kept his gaze fastened to his glass as he picked it up again and sipped from it with deliberation. Yeah, he remembered Kevin Ashland.

"Seems he always has a lot of clients on their way in, or on their way out, who needed somebody who was out, with bizness skills and a brain, to, shall we say, wash their investments clean. He takes a little somethin'-somethin' off the top for his troubles; his investors get a regular return. By way of his holdin' company, they get to show clean assets, because what flows out comes from a legit source . . . and, as they say, it's all good."

"Sounds too easy," Lem said, pushing himself upright, hailing Vivian for another round.

"If you want to play the game, you gotta learn from the experts—the white boys. This white boy is making fat bank; he's invested all throughout the hood. Does start-up capital from fifty thou up to a quarter mil. Most of the corner sub shops, bars, check-cashing joints, places located in the badlands—where only the immigrants have the heart to be, or one of us, he had a little somethin' to do with. You listening, brother?"

"I hear you," Lem said, his voice cool while his mind raced a mile a minute.

Zip downed his fresh drink, fished in his pocket, pulled out a knot held by a gold money clip, and pushed a C-note across the bar to Vivian. She smiled and stuffed the crisp hundred-dollar bill into her bra between plump breasts and waited.

"That's a helluva tip," Zip fussed. "You better clear our tab before you go pushin' that between your titties."

Vivian laughed, and retrieved the crumpled, sweaty bill. "Cheap. Just plain old cheap. See how he does me? But that's all right." Her tone was joking as she rang them up, made change, and kept what was left.

"Here's my pager and cell phone number," Zip said, leaning into Lem as he produced a business card.

Lem accepted it, and studied it hard in the dim bar light. "South Side Enterprises? Now *you* got a business card?"

Zip chuckled. "Told you I was completely legit. My attorney's number is on the left—he handles all prospective investments, or investors."

"Oh, so you also take a cut on the newbies." Lem shook his head, downed his drink, and stood. He put the card into his back pocket and nodded good-bye to Vivian, who waved.

"I'm a businessman," Zip said with a wide grin, walking him out of the bar. "It's the American way."

Bird heard her husband come in, go right to the bathroom, and shower. Acid crept up her throat. She could taste the half-eaten peanut butter cracker meld with four cups of coffee, mixed with her scant dinner. When Lem slid into bed next to her, she inhaled slowly, trying to quell the sickness. His footsteps had been easy, slow, not angry-sounding. Good. She swallowed hard again as a salty flavor added to the others that filled her mouth. And he'd lain down easy, casual;

slipped between their sheets without a word. She smelled liquor and knew he'd been drinking. Her eyes still stung from hard crying, and she felt wrung out. This was no way to live. His back was to her. Her back was to him and he didn't lean over to kiss her good night, even though she pretended to be asleep.

Whatever.

But why was her stomach acting so weird? They'd been through this type of bullshit before. When the good times were good, they were great. When it got like this, you just had to suck it up and get through it. Then one day, something would happen and he'd reach for her in the dark, and it would all be okay. That's how it always went. But, for now, she had to endure the mornings of silent vibe, the days of not being sure of where he was or what he'd be up to. The nights of no contact, no conversation, no sex—until Lem got over his shit

Whatever.

Lem lay there slowly breathing, thinking about Zip's words. *He* was the one caught up in the fairy tale, not Bird. His wife had been honest. Fact was, she didn't trust him. That was as plain as any woman could make it. She'd served truth straight without a chaser. He'd forgotten where he was from. Forgot about the double standard for a moment, and the shit temporarily messed him up. Created drama in his household that didn't have to be.

He had two choices. Go do his dream with his own resources, like a man—and stop whining 'cause a woman who had her own thing wasn't tryin' to get in the middle of it. Or settle for working for Kenny all his life—assuming Kenny allowed that. Assuming Kenny's business made it that long.

He didn't move when he heard his wife get up and go to the bathroom and shut the door. What was the point? She'd given him her back, and had pretended to be asleep. He was cut off from any nookie for the foreseeable future until he made amends. Good thing he got tightened up before the oncoming drought. She'd read him the riot act about his lack of trustworthiness, and for walking out on her in the middle of an argument. She'd have the ass when Sunday rolled around, three days from now, when it was her turn to have family dinner at this house. And he'd have to suffer through her sisters looking at him sideways and shaking their heads. Everybody would tiptoe around his bad behavior—except Teri.

He had to give it to Miss Thang. At least Teri was honest, and didn't front. Arrogant bitch that she was, she said what was on her mind. Deep. He couldn't believe that he was mentally complimenting her. Must be the Hennessey talking in his head.

Bird gripped the white porcelain sink as tiny beads of moisture formed on her forehead. Her face felt flushed as she brought cool water to her cheeks. How many more times did they have to go through this? Why couldn't things just be normal and happy? She wondered if her mother had gone through this—knowing in her heart that she must have, because she remembered her mother peeping out the window. Daddy gambled. Daddy got his drink on. Daddy loved his daughters—but had also made another one in the street before Teri, and Momma had to cope. *She* had no choice, either, it seemed.

The salty taste in Bird's mouth got thick and it was hard to breathe. She sucked in more air, and held on to the sides of the sink for support. Her stomach was doing flip-flops. Her head pounded. Goddamn . . .

If she could just breathe slowly and not pant, it might help the food settle. The cold tile floor felt good on her bare feet, almost like wet grass. She could see her father's and mother's graves, covered with cool grass. They'd stayed married for so many years, and came to rest in peace beside each other. Tears sprang to Bird's eyes and ran down her cheeks. She couldn't go there. That last resting place had been desecrated by secrets. Daddy's mistress also lay beside him, on the opposite side. That was a half sister's doing—an outside child with no moral right to lay her mother there. Nina's mother had had no right to make such a deathbed request. Just because it was legal didn't make it moral.

Secrets messed up the family, caused pain after it was too late to argue with the deceased. Maxine shouldn't have forgiven that mess. Teri should have cared more to fight it to the end. Their father had given their half sister access to the Joseph family monies. Bird sucked in more air, but it collided with food in her stomach. This is what Lem didn't understand about secrets.

She covered her mouth with one hand. Money was the leverage used to get the grave plot: give up the grave spot in the family plot, or give up a quarter of the estate—which her father had built on her mother's endurance. You didn't trust men to handle moral business. You didn't turn over your children's assets to a man to deal with—look what they did! They thought with their dicks. They had secrets, told lies. Jay would never have to see his future messed up by his father! The salon was nonnegotiable. She'd loved her father so much—but men messed up. And women endured.

Bird's stomach suddenly heaved. Her arms trembled, and her legs felt like they'd give way. She heaved again, and rushed to the john to throw up.

She couldn't live like this.

Iola Carter folded her hands in front of her on her desk and let her head drop forward. Lem understood. He knew what being disappointed was all about.

"Maybe she just needs time," Iola whispered, looking across at him. "You know," she added slowly, "in our community, it's hard. People don't take to change very well, and when you change who you are inside of a family dynamic, well . . . there's resistance."

God, he hated to disappoint this woman. She'd believed in him so much, was so damned determined—now look at her. Freakin' crushed. "You sound like some kinda therapist, not a business coach."

Iola Carter returned a sad chuckle. "If you work with entrepreneurs, you'd better be a psychologist, a marriage counselor, a doctor, and a detective, along with your specialty." Her voice trailed off and she looked up at the ceiling.

God help him, she was blinking back tears. He

looked at the tops of his Tims, noting how dirty they were from his job.

"Look..." she said on a heavy exhalation. "When people try to start a small business, everything going on in their life is a factor for success or failure. I've seen guys with good jobs and solid educations crash and burn because their significant other tripped on them—couldn't deal with the temporary loss of income, or the risk, or long hours required to launch an enterprise. I've seen people divorce over this stuff; seen people get sick—you name it, we've seen it. That's why we have to be the all-around counselor, know when people are stressed beyond the enterprise they are starting, or not eating right—whatever. If we sense it, we have to put it out there on the table, because the entrepreneur is gonna lose their dream."

She sat back and held on to the sides of her chair. Silence sat with them. He knew when someone was speaking from personal experience, and not from a textbook. This was some real shit his instructor was laying down—and to be that honest with somebody was a gift. He not only respected that, but appreciated it. And he could only wonder what scene was unfolding in her head as she'd blinked back those tears in her pretty eyes.

What brother had walked away from her or dogged her, or what enterprise did she have and lose before she had to settle for teaching others how to do their own thing? And how in God's name could she watch people come in day after day, launching the dreams they dropped in her lap, always being on the sidelines?

"You talked about family dynamics." Lem stood

and walked over to a bookcase and leaned on it. She was getting way into his head, and he needed to move. He could see Bird's expression within hers. "See, I'm upsetting the apple cart—big-time."

He was glad that she laughed. He joined her, and it felt like a pressure valve had been released in the middle of his chest. "Dig it. Kenny is the backbone—that's my brother-in-law. He's, like, the foundation. Make sense?"

"Yeah." She nodded, and made a tent with her fingers as she leaned forward again on her desk.

"When he couldn't be that for a minute, he freaked. Gave everybody the blues, until he got back his position."

"Right. People hate change, and will scratch and claw within a family to maintain their position."

Lem rubbed his jaw, and nodded. "True." He picked at a plant on the shelf. "His wife is the middle child—and the peacemaker. That's Maxine. You can count on her to hear both sides. But that makes my wife crazy."

Iola Carter just smiled. The sister was very wise not to speak. He liked that.

"Bird—Tracey—is the baby and she's used to having her way. Bird's the wild and crazy one in the bunch. Will do off-the-hook shit, I mean stuff, if you push her. Gotta handle Bird with kid gloves, 'cause she's high maintenance, on an emotional tip. You follow?"

His instructor simply nodded.

"But she's fun and lively and sexy, and really, really smart."

The expression on his instructor's face grew mellow, and her smile became warmer. "That's good, Lem."

He appreciated the fact that she seemed to like Bird.

"Then, there's Teri. She's the boss—not to be confused with Kenny, who's the foundation."

"The eldest sister, I take it?"

"Yeah." Lem sighed.

"This is the one who shoulders all the responsibility, but lets everyone know it—and as much as everyone gets pissed off at her, that's who they go to in a jam, right?"

"How'd you know?" He laughed and went back to his chair to sit down.

"Because I'm her," his instructor admitted with a chuckle. "My family stays mad at me, too. But generally I don't care, 'cause I handle everybody's raggedy business, and don't mind telling them about it."

"Deep."

They fell into companionable laughter. Iola Carter began doodling on a legal pad and then pushed it toward Lem.

"Where is Lem on this family flow chart?"

He looked at the pad for a long moment and shook his head. "That's just it. I don't fit in anywhere."

"Yes, you do," she countered. "You are the problem child. The one who everybody gets to be angry at all the time. You draw the fire, and walk point. You serve a vital function, did you realize that?"

"What?" He was on his feet again, pacing between his chair and the bookcase. "How is kicking up dust all the time a vital function?"

"With a rock and a peacemaker, a dictatorial boss and a gypsy child who needs a lot of attention, who makes the family face and deal with the tough issues that nobody ever wants to discuss?"

Lem could only stare at the woman.

"You kick up dust, Lem Van Adams. You say, do, and dredge up everybody's fears. Then a big blow-up happens, and they get to conquer whatever demons they face in the safety of blaming you. You become the scapegoat, and it's okay for them to go back to their roles. But now, you're talking about stepping out of your role."

Lem rubbed his chin. "Like, when we was rollin' as young boys, we called it peckin' order. You had to wait your turn to move up or to do a different job. You had to know your place, and if you stepped out of line, somebody would step to you—and steppin' out was dangerous. Could get a brother popped."

"Right, Lem. You're talking about challenging your brother-in-law's position as the rock, which will put him at odds with his wife. Because as the peacemaker, on this one, she's going to have to take a firm stand—which might not go over well in her domain. Very tricky situation."

"Deep." His voice was a mere whisper. The woman before him definitely had to be an old soul, no matter how young she looked. It was like talking to Momma Joe.

"Now, your wife is used to being the focus of family attention. You are about to borrow more money than she's ever borrowed in her life, your business will hit the street on a much larger scale, and all of a sudden, she will no longer be the primary breadwinner—or in total control. She won't be able to throw a tantrum and have her way simply because she owns everything by herself. The baby in the family *hates* to share. She's never really had to do it. This has got to be terrifying for her." Iola kneaded the muscles in her neck and shook her head. "I would put money on the fact that the baby in the family is tightest with the eldest sister, right?"

"Damn, you're good." He laughed.

"It's my job—and I've been studying people for a long time, Lem. The baby and the oldest are like oil and water, but codependent. The baby needs somebody to look out for her and clean up her messes and to spoil her. The oldest requires idolization and someone to follow her lead. The baby is a master at that. And, trust me, that eldest sister is going to wig out when her control of her sister's household shifts: when that baby sister is looking up to someone different, and when her word no longer becomes law, because there's a new sheriff in town—one who will hold legitimate sway, because he is an undisputable businessman. You are shaking your family up, Lem. They're not liking this at all. Right now, the oldest sister gets to put you down, talk about what you haven't accomplished, and keep her sister looking up to her. Ummph, ummph, ummph."

"This is beyond deep, sister. This is profound."

"I understand why you kept what you were doing a secret. Your gut instincts told you that derailment and sabotage was likely, and you were right on—not because your family doesn't love you, but just because.

"All of these people can ultimately be a tremendous source of support and resources. You need collateral, which you don't have on your own; and you need twenty-five thousand dollars in cash, which is partially available in your wife's business's bank accounts. You need ongoing expertise and trustworthy labor. So, what are you going to do?"

Iola Carter pursed her lips, and all but her forefingers slid from the tent they'd formed and folded together as though she were praying. The change in position created a two-finger steeple. She brought her mouth to rest against the two French manicured nails while staring at him hard. She reminded him so much of Teri, it didn't make sense.

"I guess I have to get what I need somewhere else." Lem dropped down in his chair with a thud, and looked beyond his instructor's trusting face.

"I'm going to say this to you, and I'm going to say it slowly, so we are both clear. Okay?"

The new tone that she took with him made him look her in the eyes. She was deadly serious. All fun and games had gone from her expression, there was no more philosophical vibe. He definitely saw Teri.

"I am not a betting woman, but I'd place money on it that the sources running through your head right now are *not* on the up and up."

Damn, she was good.

She let her breath out hard and pushed back in her leather chair, never losing eye contact with him. "Lem Van Adams, if you are on the straight and narrow, stay there. If I get any hint of impropriety, I will burn you—because you have burned me. With as much as I have put on the line, as much as this agency has put at your disposal, if you go left on me, brother, I will be done with you until the end of time."

He nodded. "That's fair." His voice was a hoarse whisper. "I—"

"No," Iola countered, cutting him off. "You go home to your wife. You bring her in here. You do this business right. You have us all give her the facts and details that she rightfully needs, and deserves to hear in a closed-door session, in order for her to feel comfortable enough to make a sound decision. And if she refuses, only *then* do you go looking for outside investors—and they'd better be squeaky clean, my friend."

Iola Carter stood and extended her palm to Lem, who also stood and shook her outstretched hand. "We've been straight with each other this long. I'm going to trust you, Lem. Don't burn me."

He could only agree with a nod. There was nothing else he could tell her . . . or himself.

eight

It didn't help that her husband had been nice to her all day Friday. *Shoooot* . . . After going out drinking on the heels of an argument, that Negro had *better* get up in the morning, act right, speak, and take Jay to Mrs. Jenkins, and then come home on time to bring her son home.

"Can somebody turn the heat down in here?" Bird yelled across the salon as she used the back of her forearm to wipe her forehead. Using the rattailed comb, her hands kept working with the client's hair, and she put more brown gel around the edges of it as she spoke. "Feels like the Bahamas in here, y'all. Somebody catch the heat!" Saturdays in the salon were a bitch, but a well-paying one.

"It's already freezing in here, Bird," one of the stylists protested.

Bird was about to argue with her employee about who paid for the heat they were abusing, when she noticed a rumble of agreement from her clients. Okay,

okay. Whatever. Maybe she was just warm from beating all these heads and being on her feet nonstop for hours.

As she finished the hairdo, she handed her client a mirror to check the sides and back of her head. Bird signaled to the front desk to hold up on sending the next client to her chair. She made small talk with her happy customer, and pulled the pink drape off the woman with a flair, and tossed it on the back of the styling throne. The Motrin in her system was wearing off.

Bird paced to the bathroom in her office. *Damn,* when was her period coming? She hated this bloated, tender feeling that made her jeans feel like a girdle. She washed her hands and blotted her overly warm face with a tissue, then she looked in the mirror and stuck out her tongue. It still had a yellowish-white coating on it, despite Listerine and several brushings. She just couldn't get that nasty taste to go away. More Motrin. She snatched a Dixie cup from the holder and filled it with water.

The pills hit her stomach and gurgled with the acid in it. Bird made a face, and drank down more water. It was nearly four o'clock and she'd been working nonstop since seven-thirty. She needed to get something in her system besides dry toast. Her hand went to her hair, which was dampened with sweat, and she used her fingers to lift it in strategic places without messing up her style. Then she stopped, drawing her hand away slowly to study the clump of hair in it.

She'd *kill* Leticia!

She angrily returned to the salon and walked up to Leticia, who was working on a client.

"Tish," Bird demanded in a whisper, "when you put in my color, did you get all the perm out?"

"Yeah," Leticia replied, surprised. "Why?"

"You got my damned hair falling out, that's why!" Bird fumed.

The stylist stopped working and discreetly surveyed Bird's hair. "You've got a lot of breakage, Bird," she murmured.

"I *know* that, Tish. The question is, why?"

The client in the chair was clearly listening to the hushed dispute, and Bird realized that now was not the time to argue with a stylist. Raising questions about the competency of her staff was bad for business. The last thing she needed was some sister with bad hair coming back to her salon with a lawsuit about how Cut It Up damaged her do.

"Later," Bird said in a sullen tone.

Leticia nodded, but the confused look on her face made Bird begin to wonder. Tish was one of her top stylists, and she didn't make those kinds of mistakes. Right now, clients were backing up and she didn't have time to worry about it. On top of that, her uterus felt like it was heavy enough to drop on the floor, and her lower back felt as though she were giving birth. Damn, why wouldn't her period come on and get it over with?

If her period didn't come on by Monday, she was calling the doctor to get checked out. It was time for her annual Pap smear, anyway. The last thing she needed was some kinda tubal pregnancy over the Pill, or a pregnancy at *all,* for that matter. Not with Lem acting so shaky, being salty one minute and extra nice the next. It was hard enough just to take care of little Jay. She didn't know how Maxine did it, and understood why Teri probably never would.

When Bird got up the next morning, she noticed that the house was clean. Something was definitely wrong. Her son was up, dressed, and fed, and her husband was in the kitchen. Oh, what now?

She kissed her son as she went to the table. Jay was in his high chair, having a ball playing with Cheerios on his tray. But even his cheerful face did little to improve her attitude.

"Good morning, sleepyhead," Lem said with a smile, pouring her a cup of coffee.

She accepted it and looked at the mug with suspicion, as though he might have poisoned the brew within it. "Good morning," she grumbled, and sat down heavily in a chair.

"You hungry?"

He was going to fix her breakfast? Now she *knew* something was up.

"No." She stared at him as he began to put away the washed dishes from the breakfast he and Jay had eaten. Brotherman was definitely trying to make amends. So what, that he'd been all nice when she'd come home beat last night? Who cared that he'd made her some soup when she declined his offer to go get some take-out dinner, not sure that she could even hold it down? And she wasn't giving up brownie points for him rubbing her back as she drifted off to sleep, either. That was the least he could do, after stressing her about all his business-start-up drama.

"How'd you sleep last night, baby?"

She looked at him hard. "All right," she finally muttered. She was not in the mood for small talk. Her head was pounding to the same beat as the mild cramps in her lower belly and back.

"Dinner is at our house today, right?"

He knew that, so why was he even going there? Did he want her to compliment him for cleaning up the house, *for once,* so she didn't have to do it like she always did when it was their turn to host the family dinner? Give it a rest, man. He should have been helping with that all along.

"Yeah," she finally replied with a sigh of annoyance. "I've gotta cook the chicken, and do the cornbread. Maxine is bringing macaroni and cheese and greens. Teri's bringing the dessert, as usual—because she can buy it."

"What kind of chicken you making?"

Now her husband was a culinary expert? Or, was he trying to crack on the fact that they'd been eating chicken for a week straight, and the fact that she wasn't the best cook in the family? He'd better get out of her face with that nonsense on a Sunday morning!

"Baked." She took a sip of her coffee and it didn't agree with her.

"Aw, Bird, you're not frying it?"

Fury coiled within her. "No. If you had any idea how much work frying takes, then—"

"My bad," he said, backing away from the subject. "Baked is fine, baby. I know you don't want to be on your feet all day, after being on them all week in the salon. That's cool. I like your chicken any way you fix it."

Negro betta recognize! Frying chicken was labor intensive. Men didn't know that, because they didn't do the damned work. Why did her momma even start this ritual, anyway? For once, she'd like to lie in the bed all day with the newspaper, or just zone out—no baby, no man, no pressure to cook something—nobody to interact with if she didn't want to, but her damned self.

"Well, I'm baking it, if that's all right with you."

"That's just fine," he said, going to remove Jay from his high chair. "I'm gonna take little man outside with me while I rake some leaves. I'll put him in the—"

"You lost your ever-livin' mind, Lem? It's too damned cold out there to have my son just sitting while you rake leaves!" She was on her feet now, and she didn't care if her husband or her son were looking at her like she was nuts. Hell, she *was*—they'd better leave a woman with serious PMS alone. "I'll be the one who has to take off and take care of him when he gets a cold, not you. So you put my baby in the playpen and go do what you gotta do." Shit! Lem Van Adams better not mess with her this morning. Evil was her first name, not her middle one.

* * *

If her family didn't stop talking so loudly, she was going to wring their necks. Kenny's voice hit her skull like a sonic boom, and if Maxine didn't stop hollering and barking orders, and her niece and nephew didn't stop arguing . . . if Lem didn't pick up one of those crying babies, and stop asking if she was all right every five minutes, if Teri didn't stop her incessant complaining . . . she was going to lose it. Something was wrong with her, she could feel it, but was just too weary to wonder.

Finally, they could all sit down and eat. Bird lifted a hot platter of chicken and made her way from the kitchen into the living room. As her family gathered around the table, she swallowed down the queasiness still residing in her stomach. She was definitely going to the doctor—top of the week. Soul food was supposed to make her hungry.

Lem thought about Iola Carter's words as the family took their places. Normally it bugged him when Kenny naturally drifted toward and claimed the head of the table. It was deep how, without words, everyone sat according to their pecking order, not by what was necessarily right. How could Kenny take a position at the head of the table in this house? But that was what he had to get with: this *wasn't* his house, it was the deceased Mr. and Mrs. Joseph's house, which he and Bird and his son merely occupied. The house belonged to the family, so the family sat in pecking order when they came home.

Armed with Iola Carter's insights, Lem watched the process with a new set of eyes. Kenny took the head of the table, but oddly, Teri took the foot, not Maxine. Deep. "The Boss" was just a notch below "The Foundation" in rank, it appeared. Lem also noted that Maxine sat at Teri's left hand, the argument side of things, while Ahmad sat across from his mother, not his father, and at his Aunt Teri's right hand. Oh, this was classic.

His baby niece had a high chair between Bird, who sat to Kenny's left—again, on the argument side of the table—and Maxine at the end of the table. Little Kelly was seated between him and Ahmad, which left him at Kenny's right hand.

Yeah, he was Kenny's right-hand man—always near, but not at the lead. It was as though he was seated as next in line for succession to the throne. Lem smiled as he watched his son get lowered into a high chair that was wedged in at an angle between Bird and Kenny, to Kenny's left. He wondered what that would mean? A next generation coming up strong and bogarting in? The old King Kenny better watch his back with that one—his son, Jay, wasn't going to wait to take his turn. He'd be like the young bucks, who simply took the throne when they were ready.

And though this was his space, the king got to say the blessing. This family was deep, Lem observed again, accepting and passing platters and bowls as the conversation resumed after grace.

Since he was the one designated to kick up a little dust, then he might as well begin. Lem swallowed away a chuckle with his forkful of macaroni and cheese. "This is awesome, Max. You worked this macaroni and cheese. How's the writing coming, too?"

"The macaroni and cheese is on, Max," Bird agreed, issuing Lem a glare to cut it out when Kenny bristled. Her body seemed to relax a little when their brother-in-law smiled.

"Why, thank you," Maxine replied, beaming at the compliments. "And my writing is going very, *very* well." Her tone had dropped and her gaze swept over her husband, who held on to it before looking down at his plate with a bashful expression.

Lem caught Kenny's eye from a sideways glance, and the two men shared a knowing look and a smile that went past the women's radar. Lem chuckled. No wonder the king was so cool. He'd obviously taken Lem's advice, and had probably gotten Max to try out a few of her poems on him in bed. Cool. Peace at the dinner table.

"Well, I, for one, think that Maxine's writing is a good idea." Teri folded her arms over her chest in a familiar battle stance.

Lines had been drawn. Teri challenged the king.

"Yeah . . ." Kenny murmured real slow and easy. "I like her writing."

Oh, daaaamn . . . brother had definitely scored. Lem glanced at his wife, whose fork was held in midair. He was forced to laugh out loud when all Teri could do was unfold her arms and take up a fork. Maxine's gaze connected with Kenny's down the table. The kids' heads turned from one parent to the other. Teri was pushing food around her plate. Bird put some greens into her mouth and shook her head. He could tell Teri was working on a comeback, not to be outdone by a strategic move his boy had obviously made last night.

"Well, then, Kenny, I guess you wouldn't mind if Max took a class to improve her skills, to really try to see if she can do something with this gift?"

Kenny choked on his mouthful of food and Lem slapped him on the back. The women stared at them. The children fell silent. Lem laughed again, despite his resolve not to.

"She can't have other people reading what I read last night. Uh, uh," Kenny wheezed. "That stays between husband and wife."

"Well, if her poems had that effect on you, I'm sure the public will love them. You know, black erotica is up and coming, pardon the pun."

Oh shit. Teri had pulled out the heavy artillery and had sprayed the male corner of the table. His boy had been hit, and it wasn't a flesh wound. Somebody call 911! Kenny needed cover while they dodged Teri's silver bullets. Oddly, for once, Lem found himself secretly agreeing with Teri. But just as he was about to draw on Teri out of force of habit, Ahmad provided return fire that helped Teri and his mom—not his dad. See, this was why the young bucks had to wait their turn.

"Mom is really good, Dad. Just like Reverend Pryor said in church today, 'What profit a man's soul if he gain the whole world and has not love?' Mom writes about love and stuff. You shoulda came to church with us, and you would understand."

"You've read the stuff your mother writes?"

Aw, shit . . . Kenny was nearly blowing steam out his wide nostrils, and Teri was happily eating.

There was simply no choice but to take a bullet for his nephew. "No," Lem jumped in. "I'm sure Max just told Ahmad what she writes about, or let him see some of her more mellow work, man. Nobody but you, probably, has seen all her work."

Ahmad nodded, heeding the unspoken male warning and catching on to his uncle's defense strategy. Kenny's gaze held Maxine's—which was still oddly pleasant. Then she totaled the king, just broke the man down, by smiling at Kenny. The sister might as well have rolled a Humvee over the man, the way he practically laid out at the table from her sexy glance and smiled back. The women weren't fighting fair from that end of the table. Lem shook his head. He'd been there when it was his turn.

"I didn't read him *every*thing, baby. Just the lighter stuff. *Some* things I wrote just for you."

Lem watched Kenny swallow hard. How did women do that?

Kenny started eating again, and left the subject of Maxine's taking classes alone. Bird was pushing food around on her plate, and the kids were fighting for biscuits again, trying to reach over the platters for them in the center of the table. But Lem kept his eye on Teri. She was not finished, he could tell. The matriarch would have the last word.

"Well, if you're concerned about the content of her work, Kenny, she could always publish it under an assumed name—say her maiden name, as Max Joseph.

That's a strong, regal name that could be either male or female, thus pulling in a wider audience for her writing. Frankly, I'm proud of her, just as I am proud of all my sisters in any endeavor they undertake."

"Oh . . . Lord . . . " That was the first thing Bird had said since they'd sat down.

Kenny raised his face slowly from its lowered position over his plate, like a bull that had just seen a red flag. His son didn't have the sense to pick up on the fact that his father was now El Toro. The poor boy just rushed right into the arena, no blade, no shield and no red cape, just his narrow ass. Lem tried to save the boy before he opened his mouth. "Ahmad—"

"Dad, that would be great!"

Too late. His nephew had the bull's attention.

"This way, Mom could have something of her own, like you do, with her name on it. You've got your tow trucks and your business, and she'd have her books. That would be awesome!"

Damn. Time to bring in the barrels and distraction picadors.

"Sure, everybody wants to have something they can call their own, that they can be proud of. I think that's all Ahmad was trying to say."

The bull's attention was now on Lem. If he weren't in his right mind, he'd swear that Kenny's eyes glowed.

"Well, thank you, Ahmad and Lem," Maxine added.

Lem wasn't going to let her get in here—this was no place for women and children. Kenny was cranking himself up, pawing the dirt, had lowered his horns, and was coming for the closest body. Lem needed a red tablecloth and possibly a Kevlar vest to keep from being gored. The whole thing was so ridiculous, he laughed. He'd use the truth to divert the bull.

"Kenny, man, I am so proud of you."

Kenny stopped, sat back in his chair, and tilted his head to the side.

Hell, yeah. Toro!

"You have done this family proud. Every time I drive up to the lot and see rows and rows of Chadway tow trucks there, bro, my heart fills up. A black man did that, on his own, and bootstrapped himself to a better place. Now your kids don't have to worry about the future, and your wife has the luxury of trying out the arts or running for public office, like the white boys' rich wives do."

Kenny's expression opened to a slow smile. Lem nodded, self-satisfied. Kenny reached for his hand and shook it. His sister-in-law's shoulders dropped two inches, and he got the telepathic thanks that Maxine sent down the table. He was on a roll, and it felt like the one he'd experienced at his graduation. Words could change people's lives, their direction.

"Just think, man," Lem pressed on, releasing Kenny's iron grip as he glanced at Bird. Receiving her nod, Lem continued. "Her more personal work, that'll just be for you, as a personal bonus. The other work will help build literacy in our community. Your wife might be doing book-signings and stuff which could only happen because you've afforded her the luxury to have a choice. I wanna give Bird choices like that one day, man. Give her and Jay a shot at some options—because you set the model of how to do that for a brother. Man, you're like a mentor. A good example."

He watched Kenny's chest seem to expand with pride, and was glad that Maxine kept gazing at her husband with love, and that Ahmad was now smiling at his father. Kenny chuckled and took up a fork, which meant the temporary storm had passed. But he had to get with Teri before she started something again.

"I respect you, too, Teri."

Now everybody stopped eating. She looked so stunned that it was all Lem could do not to laugh. If he'd broad-slapped her, she might not have even looked so totally confused.

"You're a good role model, just like Kenny. It's hard to be the first of anything. You're the first college grad in the family, just like your parents were the first entrepreneurs with a store. Because they set the pace, we're seated at the table with second-generation entrepreneurs, Kenny and Bird. And we might be looking at a second-generation college graduate among these kids, because of your example. If Maxine gets her thing going, she'd be the first-generation author, and one of these kids might be a Pulitzer Prize winner in generation number two. That's the thing: you never know, and that's why you've gotta recognize when somebody is the first in the line. Gotta support them. So thanks, T."

Teri smoothed the napkin in her lap and studied him suspiciously. "Thank you, I think." Then, from nowhere, she smiled.

"No, for real. This family has a lot of people who are doing right, and these kids are blessed. They're more than loved and provided for, they are nurtured and shown the way."

"Go, 'head, Reverend Van Adams," Maxine whispered.

He noted that Bird's hand shook when she reached for her glass and took a quick sip of iced tea. She didn't need to be nervous; he wasn't crazy. It wasn't rhetoric, either. It was the Gospel truth. He felt the energy at the table become galvanized, and it flowed to him, giving him the floor as the family spokesperson—he was now at the head, he was stepping up, he was setting the tone with wise words. He was king, no matter where he sat at the table.

"Kenny has built a business that is climbing fast. He and Max and their kids deserve that. Maxine is an incredibly talented woman—a great mother, and has her husband's back so that *their* business can grow. Teri is the best attorney in Chicago, I bet, and she's always been there to steer and guide everybody, and to protect us all. We are blessed. That's what we should be talking about. Not tearing down any dreams, but building them up to go to the next level. Teri has been building people up . . . she helped me and Bird get started."

"I *have* been there helping people, haven't I?" Teri's voice was filled with pride, and she sat up a little taller in her chair. "I have done my very best, and it's nice to be appreciated. Thank you, Lem." Then she did something that she rarely did—looked away.

Feeling power gaining momentum, Lem took a deep breath. Oh, yeah, there had been a shift in his position, and he'd been crowned new ruler—at least for the day.

"You have nieces who will look up to their beautiful Aunt Teri, who is sharp, no-nonsense, and who knows how to handle things. If me and Bird ever have a daughter, I want her to spend a lot of time with her Aunt Teri and her Aunt Maxine, to learn from you both. What more could a man ask for?"

Lem cleared his throat with a deep swig of iced tea as everyone simply stared at him. His gaze fell upon Bird's face and he held her eyes with his own. "But I got the best gift," he said in a near whisper. "I got the one who is a blend of all of the above. My Bird is a businesswoman, a good mother, a wonderful wife . . . and she's been there through my mess, has kicked my butt for it, but still works with me to help me get to a place where one day I might be a good role model for my son."

"Whew!" Teri finally said, breaking the silence that had fallen over the group and shaking her head while reaching for the pitcher of iced tea. "It appears everyone had a very exciting Saturday night. I don't believe I've seen near tears in my brother-in-laws' eyes in months. And I was working on legal briefs all weekend. Ummph, ummph, ummph."

The adults all laughed, dismissing the confused looks the children shared.

"I wish every family dinner could go like the one this afternoon," Bird whispered, as her finger traced Lem's bare chest.

"So do I, baby," he murmured back. She had no idea how much he wished every family gathering could go like this one had.

"You meant all those nice things you said about everybody?"

"Yeah, baby. I did. It was from the heart."

"You should talk more like that, let people know how you feel deep down inside. Then they'd be able to see more of the good man I know."

"I want you to come to the Center with me tomorrow night, Bird, when all the instructors will be there. Just give the idea a chance, and talk to the people who gave me a lot of insight—the people who helped me see some things in this family with new eyes."

She hesitated, but had not stopped tracing his chest with her finger. "You really want me to come down there and talk to those folks again?"

He chuckled from a very contented place in his soul. "At the graduation, that was chitchat, not talk. I want you to sit with my coaches and really get to understand who I was dealing with down there. Who knows? They might even be able to give you some good advice about the salon."

She chuckled in an easy, companionable way. "How do I know that you didn't just say all that nice stuff at dinner to butter everybody up?"

The erotic trail of her finger hypnotized him. "I do want peace in this family, Bird. And I do want to start a business with everyone's support—you know how you've got to warm up the clan first. But nobody would have sat there and listened if what I was saying was bogus, would they? It was all true. Truth has a way of getting people's attention."

"Then, what you said about me was all true, too . . . I mean, how you felt, and how much you respected what I'm doing with the salon?"

"Yeah." It was getting hard to think as her soft, sensual voice pummeled his senses. He could feel his eyes roll to the back of his skull as her mouth lowered over the nipple she'd been teasing, and kissed it. "Everything. . . ."

"Everything?"

"Yeah . . . everything that you do, baby . . ."

"Everything?" She giggled slow and sweet and sexy, teasing him with the mischief in her voice.

"You better stop before you start something I'll have to finish."

"Oh, yeah?"

Her palm was caressing his stomach, making it tighten.

"Oh . . . definitely . . ."

"I love talking to you like this."

"Me, too."

He loved their pillow talk, when everything was quiet in the house. Lem opened his eyes and stared up at his wife. She looked so pretty in the moonlight, like an angel. He reached up and cupped her cheek, and allowed his gaze to rove over her lemon yellow nightgown. That color was perfect for her. Soft. Nice. Like she was being to him now.

She leaned down to kiss him, and his body stirred.

His hand slid away from her face and trailed down to her breast. She stopped him.

"They're sore," she murmured.

"Oh . . . " He kissed her throat. "Near that time?"

"Yeah." Her voice was easy, and her body felt relaxed.

"Too bad. I was going to . . ."

"You can, but some places you can kiss later."

He closed his eyes as he pulled her on top of him. "How's your lower back?" he asked, rubbing it as he spoke.

"I took some Motrin," she whispered. "I'm fine."

"You sure?" He gently rolled her over and kissed her collarbone.

"Yeah." Her voice was lazy, comfortable. Her hands stroked his shoulders, then her mouth found his earlobe. "Just be gentle, okay? I'm a little tender."

"I'll be gentle, I promise." Did she know what she was doing to him? All sweet, and sexy, and the sound of her voice . . . He loved her so much that sometimes he couldn't breathe when she was in his arms. He needed to make up to her for their fight, to show her what only touch could communicate.

She missed Lem so much . . . The good side of him, that he showed her only in glimpses. The man who had stood at the graduation, the man who took charge of the family today, and settled all disputes by making everyone feel appreciated. The man who had been kind enough to clean the house, and care for their son while she didn't feel well. The man who'd gotten angry, but who came home anyway—this was the man she loved.

His breath was growing heavier with each kiss. She

For Better, For Worse

knew he needed her to be ready, but her body was strangely uncooperative. Even when she'd been pregnant with Jay, it never took her this long to feel the fire from his touch. She felt oddly distant, even though his loving was so gentle. His arms felt so comforting. They had squashed the argument, and he'd come back into the family fold.

Yet the more she felt him strain to hold himself in check, the more she just wanted him to begin and be done. If she hadn't started this, she would have curled up and gone to sleep. But she couldn't leave her husband in this state. It would be unfair and uncalled for, and might kick off a newly strained vibe.

"Baby, what's the matter?" he asked softly.

She wanted to cry all of a sudden.

"I don't know. I'm just tired. And a little tender."

"You mad at me, still?"

"No." This was not the time to have a conversation like this.

"You sure, baby?"

"I'm all right," she whispered, her hand going to her lower abdomen. "I just don't feel well."

Her husband rolled over on his back, his eyes shut tight as if he were in pain. Damn, she hated to leave him all jacked up like this—but she couldn't go on, not tonight. What was wrong with her?

"You okay?" She kissed his eyelids.

He moaned.

"Please, baby, I just need a minute. You okay?"

Her hand found the center of his chest and she planted a kiss there.

"Oh, God, Bird, stop . . ."

This was really bad. Her mind raced at options, none of them appealing to her at the moment. She didn't feel good, her stomach was upset again, and she just wanted to go to sleep. He knew that she loved him, that under normal circumstances she wanted him. She snuggled up beside him to share some body comfort, some warmth, and to convey love.

Dear God in Heaven, Lem thought. He loved his wife, but she had to understand that he couldn't cuddle right now. He knew she wasn't mad, or she wouldn't have been so sweet about trying. She was just having a rough cycle this month—probably from all the stress, and that was partly his fault, if not all his fault. He loved her more than she probably knew, which was why she had to stop stroking him, and fusing her body with the side of his.

"Bird, baby, stop. I love you, too, honey. Go to sleep."

"You want to talk about it?"

Was she nuts? Noooo, he didn't want to talk about it! Right now, all he wanted was for somebody to shoot him and put him out of his misery.

"No, baby," he said in a soft tone. "I'm tired, you're tired. Let's go to sleep. Let me just hold you." He kissed the back of her shoulder as he pulled her to him, spoon fashion. As her round backside nestled against him, he stifled a gasp of agony.

Women just didn't understand a brother's pain.

nine

Bird put the key into the front door lock, and leaned on the door as she opened it. If she didn't sit down, she was going to fall down. It was Monday evening, and her period still hadn't begun. Her hair had been breaking off badly all weekend, and she wore a headband to keep the thinning sections around her hairline from being noticed. The doctor had squeezed her in for a quick Pap smear, and told her to get some rest, and to take some vitamins.

There was no need to alarm Maxine or Teri. Once she knew a little more, she'd call them. At least she knew she wasn't pregnant—the doctor corroborated what the drugstore pregnancy test had said. It helped to have a big sister with connections; she was glad she hadn't had to wait the customary two-to-three weeks to get seen. All she had to do was make it to Wednesday, when her Pap results came back. The doctor said her period would probably begin by then, anyway.

Bird sat down on the sofa without even taking off her coat.

"Hey, baby. You ready?"

She stared at her husband for a moment as he came down the stairs. He'd obviously showered, and had put on a black turtleneck sweater and some dress slacks. She tried to wrest her mind to make sense of his question. Oh, yeah. . . . Damn!

"Baby, I don't feel up to it, seriously." She closed her eyes and leaned her head back on the sofa. "I've been on my feet all day, cramps are kicking my ass, and I just want to go lie down—I'm not even hungry."

She didn't open her eyes. He hadn't responded, which meant he was probably pissed. At the very least, she knew he was disappointed. But at the moment, she really couldn't address how Lem felt. She felt too weary to care.

"Aw'right," he said in a quiet tone. "I knew you weren't feeling well the other night. Maybe I can call them and reschedule?"

"Yeah, why don't you do that." She hadn't meant for her voice to come out so sarcastic, but he was pressuring her to deal with something she really didn't have the mental space to cope with right now.

"I know you don't feel well, but you didn't have to say it like that."

She was not in the frame of mind . . . "Where's Jay?" Again, instead of mellow calm coming from her lips, a curt question replaced it.

"At Maxine's, like we talked about this morning. I was to pick him up from Mrs. Jenkins, take him to Max's, and then we were going to go to the Center, grab some dinner, and—"

For Better, For Worse

"Okay, okay, okay. I remember."

"Guess I could have just brought him home, if you'd called me to let me know, I—"

"How many times have you been late, forgot, or gotten tied up with something and things slipped your mind? Stop *sweatin'* me, Lem. I don't feel good, okay!"

His voice had drilled a hole in her brain and a headachy throb now filled it. If this man didn't get out of her face with his mess. . . .

"Look, it doesn't have to be all of this tonight, Bird. You don't feel good. Cool. You don't want to go to the Center—cool. If you want me to make you some tea or something, then all right. But stop laying attitude and vibe down on me for no reason, or acting like I'm coming at you with a request out of the blue."

Her hands found her temples and massaged them. He was getting on her nerves so badly that she was going to snap if he didn't quit it. "Fine," she whispered. "Just fine."

"Should I pick Jay up, or call Maxine to—"

"Make the decision yourself! I am tired of having to always figure things out for you, Lem. He's your son, too, I don't feel good, and you are sweating me about dumb shit."

She was on her feet, snatching off her coat to go lie down, but he was in her way.

"You think that what I wanted you to hear about tonight is dumb shit, Bird?"

His voice was way too quiet for her liking, like a low growl from a Doberman. Was he threatening her?

"You want the truth?" She'd warned him.

"Yeah. I thought that's the new path we were on, Bird."

"The truth is, I don't care if you brought me in front of the Supreme Court, I'm not sure I'm ready to even think about parting with my salon." Before he could open his mouth to give her some rebuttal, she filled in the blanks. "I know what you are going to say: I'm not giving it up, I'm just using it to back your thing. And I know what you are also going to say about that—that all these experts agree with you, and that there is no real risk of the business failing, so why should I be worried?"

"Yeah," he murmured. "Something like that."

"Then you'll tell me that I'm unfair because I'm still judging you from the past." Her voice had become strident, and she walked in a circle while he stood by the door with his arms folded before him. The look on his face grated her to no end. "But see, that's where you're wrong, Lem. I'm not judging you on your past. I couldn't care if you had an MBA from Harvard, or whatever. I would still have these same concerns as a woman!"

He blinked twice, and looked at his wife. Had he heard her right? "What?" His voice was a mere whisper.

Tears were streaming down her cheeks now, and she wiped her nose with the back of her hand. "All of y'all lie! Teri's men did, education notwithstanding, and you have before, and so did my father! Kenny doesn't lie—he just makes Maxine swallow her dreams since his business has taken over her whole damn life, whether she likes it or not. Now you want me to give up the only thing I have to protect me and Jay in the future? Just like that?"

She'd snapped her fingers in his face and then strode away from him. "It isn't the past I'm worried about, Lem. It's the future. What, so one day my son can find out he's got a brother or a sister, and half of the business that I helped you build goes to some other baby's momma 'cause you didn't do your paperwork right? Not in this life."

He had had a lot of arguments with Bird before. Sure, they'd screamed, they'd yelled, they'd cried—but this one left him speechless. Cut past the gizzard, way to the bone, all the way down to the marrow. He could hardly breathe as she told him the honest-to-God truth. She didn't trust him not to make babies in the street on her. Didn't trust him to not leave her and their son in jeopardy. Didn't give him credit for much of anything. She sounded like a crazy woman, someone he didn't know.

He hurt so much that it was as though his soul were floating away. He was watching everything go down from an eerily peaceful distance. He heard himself utter the word "Okay." He knew his hands had reached for his coat, had dug into his pockets for his keys and produced them, and he automatically clipped his cell phone to his belt as he left, walking down the steps and getting into his car. Then he vaguely remembered turning off the radio, and riding in silence. In the far reaches of his mind, he also remembered hearing her sob, say something behind him. Maybe she'd even called his name?

He wasn't sure how he got to the posh downtown restaurant, or how Kevin Ashland came to be seated at a table with him. The only thing that was beginning to register was the dark amber fluid in his glass—Hennessey.

"So, our buddy Zip has told me a lot about you. Said you were good people, and that you and he went way back. I guess we all do, in a matter of speaking."

Lem nodded. "I understand that you finance businesses." He was in no mood for warm-up small talk.

"Yeah, a small group of investors and I have a holding company that does investments in strategic urban locations."

"I'm buying a building," Lem said, taking a healthy sip from his glass and setting it back down. "I have the mortgage covered, but it'll take two hundred and fifty to get her up to code and ready to take in shops."

"Going for broke, huh? Well . . . we can talk. The location?"

Lem looked at the man before him, his gaze taking in the expensive suit and his well-groomed appearance. For some odd reason, his mind couldn't hold the man's face, his hair color, or the hue of his eyes. He was doing a deal with the Devil, and he was strangely numbed and unconcerned about that. "The location we can discuss later, once we are sure that we will be working together."

The man before him nodded. "Are you a client?"

"You're an attorney, correct?"

"That I am," Kevin Ashland said with pride.

"Then I want to invoke client–attorney privilege."

Silence.

The man pushed back from his chair a bit and rubbed his chin with his hand. "I see you learned some stuff going through the system."

"I want to invoke client–attorney privilege. Understood? I hear you work with a lot of people—people who know some people, who can make things happen, or not happen. But what we discuss stays right here at the table."

The man nodded and smiled. "This must be very, very hot, this deal of yours?"

"It's on fire." Lem leaned back in his chair and allowed his gaze to scan the room. Unlike the other bar, people in here stared like it was okay, though it wasn't. They didn't keep their eyes moving, and it made him jumpy. He didn't like the way a young blonde kept eyeing him from across the room. "You know her, or something?" Lem tipped his chin in the direction of the young woman seated at the bar.

"Yeah. Paralegal from Green Norris. She moonlights for me from time to time when I get swamped. Feeds me tips, sends me some leads, and keeps her ear to the ground for me. A man in my business has to have a lot of eyes and ears."

That's all he needed—somebody from his sister-in-law's firm to spot him transacting business. Lem pushed himself away from the table and stood. "I'll be in touch with more details."

The man extended his hand and Lem begrudgingly

shook it, noting the wedding ring on Kevin's other hand. How could he pass the young blonde woman without conversation? This was not the kind of joint where people were cool, read body language, and would let you jet. They played mind games fronted with polite conversation.

He kept his gaze fixed on the exit as he moved across the room. In his peripheral vision he saw the blonde hop down from her stool and approach him. Yeah, Kevin was doing her. Had to be. There were no coincidences like this.

"Hi," she said brightly, "I recognized you. Aren't you Teri's brother, or something?"

Lem nodded. "Somethin' like that."

"I thought so, from the pictures on her desk of the family, and all. I didn't know you knew Kevin? You know, Kevin was with Green Norris for a while, before he went out on his own." The woman's voice had become a friendly whisper.

Lem stared at her. They weren't friends, so she needed to drop the we're-in-this-together routine. He didn't care if she was screwing some married attorney, or that she knew his sister-in-law. As a man, he could have told her that pushing up on Ashland's potential client wasn't going to make the man hang tighter to her—so she needed to go sit her ass down with Ashland, and get out of his face. He had things to do.

"They didn't give him partner, either, like Teri," the blonde went on, oblivious to Lem's vibe. "So Kevin was smart: he went out on his own and now probably makes more than all of them."

"What are you a plant, or something, to help him reel in clients?"

The young woman giggled nervously, and touched his arm. Lem looked down at where her hand landed, and she removed it.

"Kevin is really, really good at what he does. You should go with him on whatever he's proposing. He makes his clients very wealthy."

He needed to get out of there.

"So I've heard. Have a good night."

Teri sat still as Wendy Schultz rattled on, holding the picture of the Joseph family in her hand while she stood by her desk. Lem was where, meeting with whom?

"Do you know the nature of the proposal they were discussing?" Teri tried to keep her voice casual, calm, seemingly distracted. Kevin Ashland was one of the worst white-collar criminals she knew—and connected enough not to get caught. The sad thing was that she had to admit he was brilliant, in a slippery sort of way. If Lem was doing some shady deal with him, or worse.... The scuttlebutt was that Ashland had been let go for doing coke years ago, among other nefarious things. Teri steadied her nerves as the young girl rushed on. Lem was still family.

"I thought that since you and Kevin were in the same situation," she told Teri in a conspiratorial whisper, "you know, these stodgy old bastards in here wouldn't make you partner right away, like they didn't make Kevin—because he was visionary and always pushed the envelope, so I thought that if you—being so great at what you do—and he got together, especially since a family member of yours was now probably going to work with Kevin, it might be good for everybody. That's the only reason I'm telling you. Kevin could use an attorney of your caliber over at his new venture. It's taking off. He could really use you, Teri."

"I'm sure he could," Teri remarked coolly. "I'll take it under advisement, and let's keep this between us."

Women were so stupid when they were in love with an unreachable man. They'd use anything to keep him close—even their souls. Teri felt her jaw clench. The young girl beamed and set the Joseph family picture back down on Teri's desk.

"Do you want me to give you Kevin's new office number? I have it."

Teri smiled, using her most effective corporate disguise. "Yes, Wendy, why don't you do that."

She waited for the paralegal to leave her office, then studied the card in her hand as she dialed Ashland's number. If that bastard was messing with her family, or pulling Lem into some trouble, she'd have his ass disbarred. Bird had just gotten peace back into her home. Her brother-in-law finally seemed to be on the straight and narrow. All he needed was for a breeze to come by to blow his shaky butt onto the wrong side of the tracks—and Kevin Ashland was a hurricane.

As the telephone rang, she prayed that Lem hadn't done anything stupid.

* * *

"Hey, Teri," Bird said with a yawn, righting herself from the prone position on her salon office sofa. "You don't need a touch-up until next week. What brings you all the way over here from downtown in the middle of the day?"

Teri slowly sat down beside Bird. "The girls said you'd be back here. You okay?"

"I just have these cramps to beat the band, and needed to lie down for a few minutes to let the painkiller kick in."

Teri pushed a loose strand of hair behind her sister's ear, and studied her face. "Dr. Westervelt saw you yesterday with no problem, right?"

"Yeah, he squeezed me in when I dropped your name," Bird said with a weak chuckle. "Thanks. But don't worry, I'm fine, and no, you aren't going to be an auntie again—not right away, anyway."

Teri nodded. Her stomach tensed. This was the last mess she wanted to drape on Bird right now. Her sister obviously was having a bad period, since she didn't feel well enough to stand all day in the shop. But thank God it was just the normal female stuff they all had to deal with.

"You work long hours, Bird, and have a little one. Then you eat all that crazy food, or half eat it. You need to get some rest and take your vitamins, and make Lem pull more weight around the house."

Bird let out a long sigh. "You sound like the doctor—about the vitamins and rest stuff, anyway. But don't get me started about Lem."

Teri saw an in to the subject that had been gnawing in her head. "You and Lem okay?"

"You know how our relationship goes, Teri. Up one minute, down the next. We fought last week over some silly stuff, then made up over the weekend, and were back at it again on Monday night. That's why I can't get any rest."

Bird looked at her hands in her lap and folded them. This fight was way too personal to talk about while so fresh. Lem would never forgive her if this one ever got thrown back in his face by one of her sisters. It wasn't like their other debates, where there was a clear-cut right or wrong side. This was way more complicated than being angry over a man's whereabouts, or his lack of a job, things that could rally instant sisterly support.

Tears filled Bird's eyes against her will as she studied her wedding ring. She'd hurt her husband so badly that she'd drawn tears to his eyes before he'd walked out the door. And the things she said to him, she couldn't even repeat to her sister—especially because part of it related to the most painful aspects of Teri's life. The least she could do was protect them both: keep Lem's dream between husband and wife, since it wasn't going anywhere anyway, and shield Teri from what had been discussed.

Bird closed her eyes briefly, and she felt the warmth of Teri's hand cover hers.

"Have you talked to Maxine yet about how you haven't been feeling well?"

Bird shook her head no. "You know Maxine. She'd

get all worried and freak out. I did what made sense—went to the doctor, had them do my annual Pap, and then went back to work. If something is wrong, they'll call me. And since they haven't, I'm on Motrin till the curse comes and goes. I've been PMSing hard this week, girl. I'm just a little frazzled and weepy."

They both chuckled, but she noticed that Teri hadn't let go of her hands.

"Is Lem all right?"

"Lem is Lem." Bird sighed. "He'll be fine, too. Eventually."

"Bird . . . " Teri's voice held a note of concern that made Bird look up.

"Bird," her sister said more clearly, her tone more businesslike and firm, "I think he's in trouble again."

Bird withdrew her hands from her sister's hold and wrapped them around her waist as she stared at Teri. "What did he do?" Bird's voice was just a whisper.

"I'm not sure, baby," Teri replied gently. "My paralegal saw him having a business discussion last night with one of the ex-members of my law firm."

Teri hesitated, and Bird jumped in.

"Why would Lem be meeting with an attorney—somebody at the level of someone you used you work with?" Questions in her brain created a traffic jam at her lips. Maybe she'd pushed Lem too far this go-round? It might be a divorce lawyer, one skilled in custody disputes—or maybe a high-powered attorney who could go after her business in a husband and wife property dispute? She felt herself panicking, at a loss to stop the hideous thoughts slithering through her mind.

"This guy," Teri said, "is not of the caliber you think. He used to do coke, and was involved in a lot of borderline business practices that got him removed from the firm." Teri let her breath out hard. "I did some digging around, since that son of a bitch, Ashland, laughed on the telephone when I called him directly to inquire. He said Lem invoked client-attorney privilege, so he couldn't discuss it, even though I was a fellow counselor—and family member. I don't like it, Bird. Lem is a client of this bastard?"

"I don't like it, either." Bird stood slowly and walked to the water cooler. "If the guy said Lem was a client. . . . You said this guy also did coke back in the day?"

Teri nodded and then stood. "Right now, Ashland has some sort of bogus holding company. Oh, it's legally correct and very tight, the way he has it all set up. But it is ethically reprehensible. It seems he invests in businesses in the community so they can launder drug monies from ex-felons, or guys currently serving time, and then once it's clean, these people can open their own small businesses. The opening businesses part, I have no problem with. But the source of the money, and the activities that go on inside those newly opened businesses—that, I have plenty of problems with. Lem shouldn't be anywhere near those people, not when he's come so far and trying to do the right thing."

It was strange hearing her sister compliment her husband. Everything was so confused, so blurred, and changing around her so fast. She just nodded, and allowed Teri to press on.

"He concentrates on businesses in the South Side, but I also hear that Ashland is making a mint by doing this in several major cities. So I don't know what Lem is doing with this guy, or why those two ever got together, but whatever it is, Bird, you need to find out—before I do."

Nausea curdled what little she had in her stomach. "I'll get to the bottom of it, Teri. Count on it."

"What's this I hear about Lem possibly being in trouble again, Bird?"

Maxine's voice came through the receiver at such a high pitch that Bird almost dropped the telephone. Jay was wailing to get out of the high chair, and she scooped him up to settle him on her hip so she could talk.

"What did Teri tell you, Max?"

"All about this Ashland creep, and how you hadn't seen Lem since he left your house on Monday night."

"Exaggerated," Bird sighed. She had to get Maxine to chill. She was already upset enough, and Max would go off. "Monday night we had a fight, I didn't feel good, and Lem came home and slept on the couch. He was up before me and Jay, and he went right to work."

"You called the garage?"

"Yeah. And Kenny said he was there and had gone out per usual."

"Whew!"

She could hear her sister walking through her house, and she knew that Maxine had a baby on her hip, too, by the way she held two conversations at once. When Max snapped at the older children to be quiet, silence followed this time. There was something urgent, frightened in Max's voice that even the children picked up on.

"I don't want Ahmad and Kelly to hear any of this," Bird warned. "Until we know all of what's going on, we don't need the children in it—if ever."

"I know, I know, I know," Maxine fussed. "They're out of earshot. So, talk to me, Bird. What kinda mess has been going on over there between you all? As soon as Kenny comes in here, I'm coming over there, ya hear me?"

"Maxine, relax. See, this is why I didn't want Teri to even get you started."

"Bird, I'm just concerned, and I know how you are. You hold things in, don't tell people until the last minute, when things get out of hand. Then it's a crisis. If Lem is in some pending crisis, then—"

"What if I'm the one in a crisis, Maxine? What if I'm the one who is scared, worried sick because I'm not sure of what's going on, huh? Forget what Lem's going through. What about me? He's at work with Kenny for now, and is safe. But I don't know what my husband might have done, and I'm scared."

Bitter sobs replaced her angry words. She could not go into the details and jeopardize her husband's job, or his relationship with Kenny. She couldn't tell her sister that Lem might have gotten himself into a mess with shady investors—so he could leave his job, leave Kenny in the lurch, and put the Chadway household at risk financially, because the towing company would be short its best man. And how could she explain to Maxine that she'd known about Lem's building plans, but hadn't told her about a project that would affect the Chadway house? She wasn't even sure if that was why Lem was with Ashland. Hell, he might have been there starting divorce proceedings, for all she knew!

"Bird, Bird," Maxine repeated into the receiver, "please, honey, what is going on with you two?"

The more her sister asked, the harder she cried. Her son was wailing away, too, upset that his mommy was so upset. Guilt tore at Bird's insides. Her sister loved her, and her man wanted things from her, too—and she couldn't disclose what she needed to say to either of them.

"We're coming over, Bird. And, I'm calling Teri."

Kenny set the telephone down slowly and stared at it. His hands found his face and he rubbed his palms down it in frustration. What had brotherman done now? Jesus H Christ. The Joseph women had posseed up. Teri was on an investigative manhunt, Bird was in tears, and his wife was in a minivan going to the rescue with children in tow to drop off at a neighbor's before a sho'nuff fight.

He found the dispatch microphone and called Lem in. It was time for his brother-in-law to talk to him, before things got out of hand.

Twenty minutes had never seemed so long, and Kenny stood as Lem walked through the door.

"Yo," Lem said. "You paged me *and* called me to

get back here, and I was way 'cross town. Whassup? One of the crew break down here and need a jump or something?"

"Sit down, Lem." Kenny took the edge of his desk as a perch.

Lem leaned against the door and declined the command to sit.

"What is going on with you these days?"

Lem stared at him.

"I'm serious. What is going on with you and Bird that has all three women at your house right now in a powwow, brother? If you're straight, I got your back."

"Me? Me! What's wrong with me? And you say *if* I'm straight? Don't you freaking know if I'm straight by now, brother-in-law?"

Anger ripped through Lem with such visible force that it made Kenny stand.

"Hey, hey hey . . . I'm not the enemy, brother." Kenny had put his hands up in front of his chest.

"Oh, right. You're neutral. You're Switzerland. Just asking questions. Right."

"Whoa." Kenny walked closer to Lem. *"What is up?* Talk to me."

Lem paced away from him. He needed space and Kenny was hemming him in. He needed to keep moving. "You wanna know what's up? First try having your wife tell you that she don't trust you for nothing, with nothing—no matter what you do or what you say. If Maxine came at you like that, you would be done, Kenny. *Done.* You can't even handle the woman wantin' to take a class—if she told you something like what Bird told me, you'd have a damned heart attack!"

"Okay." Kenny's voice had gone analytical, calm, like a hostage negotiator trying to appease a cranked-up kidnapper on the edge. "But we ain't talking about Maxine and me. We're talking about you and Bird. What is going on?"

Lem looked at the file cabinets and clenched his jaw.

"All right. Not talking. Cool," Kenny said with a long sigh. "Then let me tell you what they are cooking up to beat you down with when you get home, man. Apparently, Teri said she got from a reliable source that you met with some guy, Kevin Ashland, who does laundering investments. You following me?"

"I'm following." Lem kept his gaze away from Kenny's and neither confirmed nor denied the charge.

"Well, the women got concerned, because this guy not only finances shaky deals, but used to do blow and rock—"

"Oh, so now I'm dealing again! It always gets back to that, doesn't it?"

"Look. I'm not making accusations. All I'm saying is we both have a new chance, Lem. You got a chance to go straight, and I've got a city contract that cannot come near any—"

"I do not believe I am hearing this *bullshit* from my family, from you!" Lem was now walking in a circle, breathing hard, hitting the wall as he passed between the door and the file cabinet and back.

"Kenny, first of all, I ain't dealing. Second of all, I went to Ashland as an investor for a legitimate business situation—since Bird told me that under no circumstances, even if I graduated from a Big Name College, would she consider me, or any man—like I was *any* man and not her husband—worth the risk to commingle finances. So when you say you want to have my back before I go home, truth be told, I ain't *got* no home. That ain't my house—it's the Joseph house, owned by the Joseph sisters, and I'm a black mother who happens to crash there upon occasion. Kiss my ass, Kenny. You don't know nuthin' about any of this!"

"What business, Lem? What business that you couldn't come to family with to discuss, to finance, to help you get up and off the ground?" Veins were standing in Kenny's neck now, and his gaze was trained on Lem for a showdown.

"Come to family?" Lem shook his head and gave a hard chuckle. "I *went* to family. My wife. I brought her to my graduation from business classes—from a legitimate agency. *Twelve weeks.* Yeah, that's where I was. I even got a certificate, if you won't take my word. And I asked my family, my *wife*, to have my back. I was trying to come correct, and I asked her to invest with me in my dream: not some fly-by-night shit, but something that top finance people had reviewed. Something banks were considering. And she told me to stop wasting her time."

"Why didn't you come to me, man?" Kenny's voice had de-escalated to a murmur.

"Every time I did, and I tried to talk to you, the Chadway Towing thing was over my head, hanging 'round my neck like a noose—and you of all people should understand what it's like to have your own ideas burning in your brain. You're my brother-in-law, and my friend, but also my boss . . . and I didn't want to let you down with your big break. But I need mine, too. So I went to some people who know some people, after going the family route fell apart."

Lem waved his arms out in front of him. "This is what I get for going to class for twelve weeks to better myself. And *this* is what I get for going to my wife, asking that she keep our private conversations between us, within our own bedroom. And *this* is what I get when I say to hell with it, and I go find other aboveboard sources of financing outside the family."

Kenny opened his mouth to speak, but Lem cut him off.

"You know why, brother? Because Lem Van Adams has a past, is not to be trusted, and is not respected by a soul in this family. Not even you."

"That's not true, man."

Kenny's hoarse whisper held him ransom for a moment. But he shook it off.

"It is true," Lem replied, fatigue now flowing through the veins where adrenaline had just rushed. "Sad, but true. Because you almost said to me, 'Lem, my new contract has to be cool, and if you got some mess with you—not here.' You were going to tell me about your wife and kids, and all that you had worked hard for, like I didn't know those things. And you were going to tell me about not being willing to risk that, even though you loved me like a brother. Just like my wife looked me in the eyes and said those things to me."

Lem swallowed hard, and glanced away when Kenny couldn't answer him.

"Maxine will never say those things to you, or believe those things about you, Kenny." His voice was a whisper of calm resignation as he told Kenny the truth. "You're a blessed man. And until you've walked a mile in my shoes, don't judge me. Don't tell me to suck it up and let it rest. And don't tell me where to go to finance my dream to be my own boss."

He turned on his heels and left. Cold air slapped his face and stung the water in his eyes. He found his car in the lot, and it found its way to old roads that they both remembered by heart. The street called his name soft and gentle, and knew who he was. The streets didn't judge; they just were.

It was *definitely* all a matter of perspective.

ten

"So what exactly does all this mean, Dr. Westervelt?" Bird sat on the edge of the examining table, her gaze riveted to the fluorescent pads on the wall that held black-and-white pictures of her insides. Chilly air slid down her back through the gown opening, and her arms wrapped around her middle to protect herself from the doctor's words as much as from the cold.

With his gaze trained on the wall, Dr. Westervelt addressed her. "You have multiple, significant fibroid tumors pressing against your fallopian tubes and adhered to your left ovary." He paused, and adjusted the half glasses on the bridge of his nose. "There are masses within your uterus. From the ultrasound, we can surmise that these are also fibroids—but the Pap results concern me, as do your other symptoms."

His words echoed in her mind and made her feel clammy all over.

"Okay. Okay. Then what happens next?"

The doctor looked at her, his eyes concerned, his voice firm. "We need to biopsy the masses, Mrs. Van Adams. That's why we called you in to get an ultrasound in here today, rather than just giving you the Pap results over the telephone."

"A biopsy? But I thought you said the masses were just fibroids."

He held her gaze. "Whenever there are masses present, we want to be sure."

Silence.

He wanted to be sure.... Bird covered her mouth and her body rocked on the edge of the table so subtly that she wasn't even aware that she was doing so until the nurse touched her shoulder.

"This could be cancer?" The big C; every woman's nightmare. She closed her eyes as tears filled them.

"Let's not be hasty," the doctor said reassuringly. "In all likelihood, it's just a significant fibroid presentation. We cannot tell from a mere ultrasound though, and even blood work can be spotty, so I need to go in there and have a look."

"Surgery?" Bird wasn't sure if she'd actually whispered the question or if it was just contained within her skull until the doctor answered.

"I'd like to get you prepared for the procedure as soon as possible. I'll have the nurse set it up, and when you get dressed, we can talk more about the alternatives."

Alternatives? "Doctor, wait. What alternatives?"

Dr. Westervelt paused. The small ellipsis of time was enough for horrible visions to careen through

Bird's mind. She saw her skin gray, taking chemotherapy, covering her head with wraps and wigs. She saw large scars on her abdomen, which would be emptied of its female organs, hollowed out. Then she saw a grave—her son and her husband laying flowers upon it.

"Let's not jump to the worst case and become alarmists. We need to stay calm."

We, hell!

"During the procedure, I'll go in and remove the fibroids. While you are under anesthesia, we will send tissue samples up to the lab. If all is well, we will simply remove the tumors in a myomectomy procedure. You'll be fine in a matter of weeks, the hormone fluctuations should abate, and you will be able to go on and have more children." He paused. "However, if the lab results are not what we'd hoped for, then I may need to do a partial or full hysterectomy—depending on what we find when we go in there. Once you get dressed, have the nurse bring you into my office, and I'll have some brochures on these various procedures for you to take home and discuss with your husband." Then he nodded to the nurse and was gone.

Hysterectomy? She was to take that information home to her husband? A man who didn't come home last night. A man who hadn't gone to work, and was nowhere to be found. The person who'd be laying flowers on her grave with her son. Bird felt her shoulders shake as she covered her face with her hands. The nurse told her to take as long as she needed. What did time mean now? She'd squandered so much of it on drama. It wasn't fair. Things like this were not supposed to happen to people. Not to her. Not to any young woman.

She wasn't even thirty years old.

"Maxine, baby, I know. No," Kenny whispered into the telephone from his desk. "I don't know where Lem is. No, honey." His wife's hysterical voice filled his ear, and he tried to remain calm, tried to draw upon the Wisdom of Solomon to allay his wife's worst fears. "Yes, baby. I promise. I'll go out and look for him. Yeah, yeah, Francis can cover the telephones and do dispatch. You got the number to that Center he was going to? Try there while I'm in the street."

Lem sat up slowly, allowing his mind to comprehend his surroundings. He glimpsed the cheap clock radio on the nightstand beside him. Damn! He'd have to pay for two nights instead of one. It was way past noon—checkout time. His head throbbed with the residual effects of spending the night with his own personal bottle of top shelf.

The sight of the grubby truck-stop motel room made him want to hurl. Stumbling to the bathroom, he left the light off. His eyes couldn't stand high-beam fluorescent. His nervous system was fried. No stimuli this morning—or afternoon, as the case may be.

He somehow made his way over to the tub faucets and began turning the creaky knobs. Soon a hot jet sprayed from the showerhead, and he stepped into it on wobbly legs. Coffee. He needed java. He hadn't been this tore down in a long time and needed to get something into his stomach before he faced the music. They'd all be waiting for him, ready to jump on him. Ready to kick his ass. But liquor had beaten them to the punch.

Still unsteady, he made a dripping trail to gather the heap of clothing in the middle of the floor. When he bent to collect them, his brain caught fire in his temples, sending a searing throb to stab him in the back of his eyeballs. "Never again," he whispered. He didn't know how he used to do this and call it fun, when he was younger. He was lucky to still be alive. This was crazy. He was married.

Married. Lem hit his cell phone On button and squinted as the blue-green light came on on the faceplate. Everybody and their mother had tried to reach him, it seemed. That doggone Joseph-Chadway clan was a bunch of drama addicts. He'd be back in their clutches soon enough. Right now, he had one objective. Coffee.

Bird parked in front of Victory Bible AME. Her legs propelled her up the massive white steps to ring the bell. She said a small prayer of thanks that it was Wednesday, and there would be someone there to unlock the doors for midweek Bible study.

"God bless," came the church secretary's warm welcome through the intercom. "May we help you?"

"Yes, Sister Williams. It's Tracey Van Adams. I was wondering if Reverend was there this afternoon, and if I could come into the church for some prayer?"

"Oh, certainly. The church and our Reverend are always here for that."

The buzzer sounded and Bird leaned against the door, turning the knob to enter.

She knew Reverend Pryor would be in his office waiting for her, but she wanted a moment alone with the Lord before she spoke to anyone else. She thanked God that the sanctuary was empty when she entered it.

Bright rays of color poured through the stained-glass windows, adorning the pews in rich blues, reds, and golds. She picked out the place where her mother always sat. It was bathed in gold.

She slid into the seat and hot tears of remembrance filled her eyes again. Where was her mother now? Why did God have to remove a saint from their midst? She slid down to kneel. Her hands clasped each other and her eyes squeezed shut, pushing out more tears. Her head found her fist, and her mind tried to lock on to a beam of light to send up her prayer.

"I'm not questioning you, Lord, or challenging you," she whispered. "I'm just asking for you to be with me. Help me, Father God, because I am afraid."

She had a little baby boy. She wanted more children. She was a young woman. She wanted her marriage to work. Please, God, don't let them carve up her body. Vanity was a sin, she knew that, but she confessed her fears as a woman nonetheless. She wanted to still be pretty, to have hair, to not have to take hormones so that her chin would not sprout hair, her breasts would not sag, and her insides would not be dry to her husband's touch. She told God all, for he already saw all. He knew her heart; he knew what she could not form on her lips to say to him.

When a strong hand splayed against her back, she leaned into it and turned to arms she'd grown to trust as a little girl. Her head sought Reverend Pryor's shoulder as his voice repeated, "Shhhhh, child, he hears you. Let it out. Bring it to Jesus and lay your weary burden down." Those arms in a black robe rocked her. The hand that stroked her head did not require that she explain. He just rocked her, and soothed her soul.

After a long while, a stillness came over her. Her breaths more steady now, she slowly pulled away from the arms around her. A kind face looked back at her, and a warm smile greeted her.

"Thank you, Reverend Pryor," she whispered. "I'm sorry I just lost it in here like this. I haven't been coming regular, I know, but—"

"Child," he said in a soothing voice, covering her clenched hands. "Oh, child . . . don't you know that when God wants you to come to him, he'll bring you to him? Wherever and whenever that might be. And my job, as your pastor, is to be here when one of his flock come in search of his voice. You are never out of the fold, as long as you believe."

"I've done some awful things, said some awful things," she said hoarsely. "And now . . ."

"Whatever you did, you are not being punished," he murmured. He handed her a tissue from a box that he'd brought with him from his office, somehow knowing that he'd need them if he found her in there.

"Our Lord is a loving God. Forgiveness is divine.

Use whatever trial and tribulation that sent you in here to repair the damage, to open your heart, and to be as forgiving to others as you have been so forgiven." The minister's gaze held hers with a calm sureness. "I might not have seen you in a month of Sundays, but I am not to judge—for he who is without sin, let them cast the first stone. We all have stumbling blocks in the road, but we must examine our hearts and stay on the path." Then he smiled.

She nodded and squeezed the strong, dark brown hands that clasped hers.

"I have so much to learn," she whispered.

"As we all do, those of us still living. He has taken his saints, like your mother, on to Glory. We all stumble and fall and scrape our knees. That is the human condition. We all need someone to believe in us, to lift us up, and to help us try again. Sometimes people fail, but God will not."

His kindness and mercy washed over her, giving her spirit absolution.

"Thank you so much, Reverend," she said.

"Shall we have a little prayer before you go off onto the path of life again? Something to send you on your way in safety and in good spirit?"

"Yes," she murmured. "I'd like that—I need that." He had unconditionally accepted her into his arms. He hadn't asked what was wrong, didn't need to know where she was coming from, or where she was on her way to next. She'd sobbed like a baby, and he didn't ask her why. All he did was open his arms and accept her where she was right now. "Thank you."

"Then let us bow our heads and ask Father God to send angels of healing and mercy and protection to watch over you as you move through this world, and to spread those blessings over your husband and your child and over your entire family. Let us ask for peace to be restored where there has been contention. Let us ask for healing to take the place of any sickness. Let us ask for abundance where there has been lack or want. And let us ask for this blessing to be sealed in Our Father's name, in accordance with his promise and His divine will—we are his children and inherit only that which is good and right, as we, the church, say amen."

When Bird entered her home, her living room was filled with concerned family members. Her two sisters sprang from where they had been sitting on the sofa and rushed to her for a three-way embrace. She noted that Kenny stood slowly, abandoning his chair, his expression solemn—as if he had failed.

"I tried to find him, Bird . . . to let him know what was going on. But I couldn't."

Flanked by her sisters, Bird went to her brother-in-law and touched his cheek. No words were necessary as she hugged him, and his big bearlike grip encircled her with affection.

"Baby girl, I am so sorry," Kenny whispered. "I'll keep looking all night and all day till I find him."

"It's all right, Kenny," she told him, feeling Maxine's grip about her shoulders tighten in support.

"He will come home. That's when I'll talk to him."

"Bird," Teri began, dropping her hold, "he should be here now! I cannot believe this." Sudden tears had filled Teri's eyes and she wiped at them angrily.

"Teri, chill," Maxine ordered, leaving Bird's side and going beneath Kenny's arm. "Just stop it. Now is not the time. I know you're upset; we all are."

"Hold on, hold on," Bird said quietly, making everyone pause. She went to Teri and gave her sister a hug. This time it was not a hug for self-comfort, it was to offer love to a woman who stood before her very afraid.

"Oh, Bird . . ." Teri's face went into Bird's hairline. "It's just not fair, it's just not." Teri's voice broke and shattered into quavering breaths as her resolve to not cry edged away from her.

Bird rubbed Teri's back for a while, knowing her sister felt mortally wounded. She was used to being in control, but now something too big to control had threatened one of Teri's own—and for once, there was no court to argue the case. There was no answer. It just *was*, and there was no choice but to wait it out, see what the doctors would find. Bird allowed her sister to weep out her tears of frustration upon her shoulder, knowing what it meant to carry a weary load for a long time. And as she stroked away the pain, her hand transmitted unconditional love. It was a gesture so basic, so fundamental, that it drew Kenny and Maxine to gather around them.

They stood in the middle of the floor like that for a long time until Teri's quiet sobs abated.

"You can't fix everything, Big Sis," she whispered,

wiping tears from Teri's streaked face and kissing her cheek. "Don't be angry at her, Max," Bird urged as Maxine touched Bird's hair. "You know our sister's way is to fight it. To come at everything hard with aggression, and kick its butt before it kicks hers."

The others gave a tension-relieving chuckle.

"But, Teri, sweetheart," Bird whispered, "sometimes your arms are just too short to box with God."

"How'd you get so wise?" Maxine murmured, hugging her again. "You're supposed to be the baby in the family, and we're supposed to be telling you these things."

"I learned by getting my ass kicked." Bird chuckled. "I found out who was really in control out there."

Maxine just shook her head and went back to Kenny's side.

"I'm going to keep looking, Bird. You can count on me."

"Kenny. No." Bird's voice was soft, tender, as she looked up at the family's gentle giant. "Don't feel bad because you didn't find him. You weren't supposed to. He is supposed to come home on his own, when he's ready."

"But what about all the secrets, the lies, and this crazy business scheme? Bird, please!" Teri shrieked, losing her momentary calm.

Bird gave Kenny and Maxine a warning look.

"The past, Teri." Her voice was calm, resolute, the way she'd seen her mother handle her sister. It was as if a part of her mother's DNA took over her own, and her mother's tone replaced her voice. It made Teri stop and turn around. It held the peace and stabilized the room.

"His ideas were not necessarily crazy. They were dreams. His hurt was real, but what happened between us pales in comparison to what we might be up against. And there will be no more secrets—the family will be told all in due time. But when that man walks through the door, if you are here, you let *me* handle it. You let *me* address *my* husband's behavior. You let me work it out with him. Are we clear?"

"Well . . ."

"Teri, I am very serious about this. There are things that go on between a man and wife that nobody knows. And it is all a matter of perspective."

"I just don't want you to get hurt," Teri whispered. "Oh, Bird, you just don't know how much I don't want that to happen."

"And that's why I love you so much, and put up with your way of fighting the world for me. But this is my battle, and I am not going into it blinded by love, or my own personal demons." Bird walked to her sister and pushed a wisp of hair away from Teri's cheek, noting the tension in her carriage, and the way her sister held herself tall, thrusting her chin up as though daring the world to challenge her.

"Remember when we were kids, y'all?" Bird chuckled. She took her time, allowing her sisters to go back in time, watching their faces transform as their expressions relaxed. "Teri learned how to ride her bike first, and busted up her knees real bad. So she wouldn't let

Maxine ride without running beside her, telling her where all the cracks were on the pavement. She crowded Max so bad that Max fell and bumped into a tree and split her lip."

They all laughed at the easy memory. Teri smiled and Maxine shook her head.

"Yeah, Bird. She was so close to me that I had a choice of running over her, and making us both fall, or going into the street. The tree was in the way, and next thing I knew, boom, I was down."

"Yup," Bird said with a smile. "Then when it was my turn, both of y'all were on either side. And Momma was watching from the window hollering instructions about how not to let me fall, don't let me go into the street, don't let me skin up my knees. I was a basket case. Didn't even want to ride my bike, and came in the house crying. Then, after y'all had scared me to death, you called me a baby."

"I remember that," Maxine murmured, her gaze going to the pictures of the family on the mantel.

"So do I," Teri whispered.

"Let me ride this bike," Bird said quietly. "I will not go into the street. I will not hit the tree. I might fall down and skin both knees—and if I do, and come in crying, you can put Bactine and Band-aids on them, then."

"You'll let us know if we can do anything, right?"

Yes," she told Maxine. "Your watching Jay for a little while is a big help, and that's all I need right now."

"But, please, Bird," Teri pressed on. "Just tell me that you are not considering whatever wild business idea Lem has, that you're not going to jeopardize the salon or your part of Momma's house—especially if, God forbid, you get sick. It's not likely, but you always have to prepare for the worst. You've got to protect your son with an ironclad will before you go into surgery."

Her sister was being real, coming from a place of concern. Yet the momentary silence was deafening.

"Good Lord, Teri," Maxine said. "You're overreacting."

"We do have to talk about it, Maxine." Bird said. "Teri is right, I do need to get a will done. We all need one, and it's something we all avoid talking about. Tomorrow's not promised, at any age."

"You're right. Still." Tears filled Maxine's eyes.

Teri came to help Maxine sit on the sofa, then sat down and hugged her. Kenny hovered nearby, looking bewildered. Bird's family was reconstituting itself, shifting its alignment and foundation points.

Quiet descended upon them again. They had all tasted pain at some point, but it was nothing so deeply personal as this. During the car accident, they had all been injured either in body or spirit, or both. But there was no hurt deeper than to have to stand by, helpless, with only blind faith to carry you through.

Coffee never tasted so good. It was like morphine. It began to clear Lem's head and take away the pain. Eggs and grits and toast formed a base within his stomach. His brain was coming alive again, his senses returning, reality settling in once more.

He looked up and hailed the waitress at the diner. "Keep the coffee coming, Sis."

She nodded. Must have seen men in his condition before; there were plenty around here.

His hand raked across the excess stubble around his normally neat beard. Damn, it was practically dinnertime and he was just coming alive in the world and eating breakfast—like a vampire, coming out as dusk settled into night. This bullshit didn't make sense. Nothing was worth living like this.

He pulled his cell phone off his belt and looked at the calls registered on it again. Home, the garage, the Center—those numbers appeared multiple times. Seventeen calls?

Panic seized him. What the hell had he been thinking? What if something was wrong with his son! His fingers punched in the voice mail code, and he waved the waitress away when she brought a fresh pot of coffee to his table. Bird's message sounded like she'd been crying. She just told him to come home. She didn't leave details, didn't elaborate, but sounded frantic. Russell Hampton from the Center said there was an urgent call from his family. Teri had left a strident message that there was a family emergency—"Get home." Kenny had hollered at him to "Come back to base camp, soldier." Maxine sniffed out her message about all hell breaking loose. Then the series repeated again with more urgency, like a nightmare spiraling out of control.

He was instantly on his feet, dropped a tip, paid the bill, and was gone.

When he came into the house, his wife was sitting on the sofa in the dark, curled beneath a blanket, staring out at nothing.

"Where's Jay?" The door slammed behind him and he rushed over to grab Bird by both arms. "What happened?"

"Jay is at Maxine's for a while."

Her voice was too calm. He was losing his mind.

"Why didn't you pick up the telephone? I kept calling on my way here, and nobody would answer it."

She didn't speak for a moment. He wanted to shake her, but didn't.

"Max, Kenny, Teri . . . is everybody all right?"

"No, they're not," she whispered. "They are all worried to death, but are managing."

"The children . . . dear God, Bird. The children?"

"All okay, and safe, Lem."

"Then what's wrong!" He closed his eyes and raked his fingers across his scalp in frustration.

"Take off your coat and sit down. I have something very important to talk to you about, and it can't be like this—all hyped."

He hesitated. Something about the way she was so calm, so peaceful, told him that this was serious. So serious that she didn't spring it on him with her hands on her hips. She hadn't met him at the door with accusations, nor had she run to him to fill his arms, sobbing from some temporary upset. This was big-time, serious.

He took off his coat and sat down and waited.

"I went to the doctor's today."

The muscles in his chest constricted around his heart.

"They found something, Lem."

Words lodged in his throat and blocked his ability to breathe.

"I have to have surgery."

He'd heard what she'd said, but his mind needed more sentences, more pieces to the puzzle.

"Maxine is going to watch Jay while I'm gone, and depending what they find, then we'll go from there."

His memory locked on to her pain when she'd made love to him, the fatigue, the irritability. "Oh, baby . . ."

"I'm sick, Lem."

She looked at him, her eyes glistening in the darkness. Moonlight hinted at the salty remains of a steady quiet stream that flowed down her face.

"I have masses inside my uterus, and around my tubes and ovary. They don't know what it is. They might be able to get the fibroids out, if that's what they are. But if it's more than that . . ."

His arms reached out and her body offered no resistance as she filled them. He kissed the crown of her head, and pulled her against his chest. "It'll be all right, baby. I promise."

"That's not your promise to give, baby," she whispered back.

He knew that, but somehow hearing her say those words made him feel so utterly powerless. He closed his eyes as his lips met her hair again. Tears ran down the bridge of his nose and fell into her soft curls. He sniffed them away quickly. She needed him to be cool, to be strong, to have an answer.

Yet, never in his life had he felt so helpless—only during the time when she'd been injured before. But that was different: a sudden trauma, something the doctors had rushed in to fix, and then sent his baby home. But masses took life like a thief in the night. Doctors couldn't sew up or patch those demons. There were no scalpels that could enter something wrong with the blood, to reverse the damage if it had gone too far.

"Jesus . . . " He rocked his wife as his throat constricted. "Tell me what to do, Bird. What are the doctors saying has to be done?"

Although she explained all the details that she knew, his mind scavenged memories. All the time that they had wasted fighting about nonsense. All the years that might be robbed from them, if this thing didn't go right, if they hadn't caught this monster in time. All the nights they'd gone to bed not speaking to each other, instead of cherishing what they had.

"I have to draw up a will, Lem."

"It's not that bad yet, is it, Bird?" Panic made his voice stumble and fall upon a whisper.

"I don't know. We won't know till they go in and get results from the lab while I'm on the operating table."

"Oh, shit . . ." He stood and walked across the room in the dark. He wrapped his arms around himself and kept his back to her. He was supposed to be strong, not let her see him sob. He would take this like a man. He drew in a ragged breath and remained with his back to her, trying to collect himself for her.

He heard her stir, but he could not turn around. To his amazement, he felt her hug his back, laying her damp cheek against his spine. He breathed in sharply. No, he *would* not cry. His woman needed him to be the strong one. To suck it up, and take the bad news like a man.

"Realities like this give you a lot to think about."

He could only nod as she took his hand and led him to the sofa again.

"I got to thinking about the past . . ."

He closed his eyes and allowed his head to lean back. Memories of the things he'd done, and left undone, stripped him naked and lacerated him in the quiet.

"We all have a past," she murmured. "The past things I've seen made me afraid—but until this moment, I didn't really know fear . . . fear that was so paralyzing, it makes you get still. Do you understand?"

He nodded. In that moment, he knew exactly what she meant.

"I got to thinking about Jay. And thinking about him made me realize how afraid I'd been for his future, all because of the things I'd seen other people, like my father, do. And I measured you by those fears from the past, and didn't trust you not to hurt our child. But if I'm not here on this planet, who will raise our little boy?"

"Don't talk like this, Bird. You're scaring me."

"That's the first honest thing we've said to each other, really. Do you realize that, Lem? Me telling you it wasn't just you, and you telling me how absolutely afraid you are about all of this right now."

He opened his eyes and stared at his wife. Somehow she'd become someone he didn't know. Someone wiser, more sure, and with a tone so calm that it was chilling, she was telling him things that made him want to beg for mercy.

"Lem, I was afraid of sharing the salon *not* because it was you, but because of what it represented to me."

"I don't care about the salon, or some stupid dream—not in comparison to this." How on earth could she could think he was still fixated on something so remote at a time like this?

"No, hear me out," she whispered, pressing her fingers to his lips. "People go out of this world every day, without bringing closure to issues with the people they love. And those people are left alive, but hemorrhaging to death, from unfinished business. So I want to resolve these questions that have been haunting us. Please let me, Lem."

What in God's name could he say to that? He nodded and let her speak.

"I think your idea is a good one. But I want to be sure that the salon is covered by a will if you use it as collateral, either now or in the future. Not because I don't love you, but because I am a realist, and I know that your life is gonna go on, even if mine might get cut short."

"No, baby . . . don't go there." The truth she told

pierced the very core of him, turning a blade in his chest that nearly stopped him from breathing, it hurt so much.

"There was a man who loved me more than life itself. My father. He loved all of us that way, especially our mother. But unfinished business hurt us so bad, Lem; I can't even explain it. That's what makes me want to ensure that our son, the only baby I may ever have, will be made safe from that kind of pain—no matter what."

"Then let's do that. Whatever you need, to know that Jay will have everything we've got to give him—every opportunity."

"Which is why I want you to do the presentation for the family—over at the Center, Lem."

He raised his head slowly, disbelief leaving him dazed. "What in the world are you talking about, Bird? Like I give a rat's ass about some stupid building at a time like this? Do you think I'm that low, that—"

"I think you are that capable, that honest, *that* worth hearing. I don't care if you decide to chuck your project, or go forward with it. I want my family to know who you are, to see your intelligence and honesty. So that if I go out of here, there won't be any bullshit with my sisters fighting with you over Jay. I'm putting that clearly in my will. My son stays with his father: a man worth raising my boy. Our son, not theirs. And I trust that you will never put him in a situation that harms him or separates you from him, no matter what. No other children, no new woman, no job, no crime, no nothing. Do you understand me?"

She'd given him something of much greater value than collateral to back a business. She'd given their son over to him—a gift worth more than life itself. And she'd said it so calmly, so matter-of-factly, like it was something he should have known all along.

At the time when she should have been most afraid, and trusted him the least, she'd just given him the most. *The last shall be first and the first shall be last* . . .

His hands became blurry as a soft touch alighted on his shoulder. His nephew had told them at the table, "What profit a man's soul if he gain the whole world and has not love?" Pure wisdom from the mouths of babes. Bird was his soul. Jay was his spirit.

Hot blotches hit and splattered the tops of his shoes. Streaks of wetness burned his cheeks. Bird's arms held him and began to rock the pain up from the depths within him. Pain he'd buried from his childhood, pain from not having the arms of a wise mother to touch away the hurt. Bird found his tender center, vulnerable to the outside world, and had peeled back the tough layers of protection to find the root of the wound.

She tapped that vein of deeply concealed hurt, beyond layers of man-pride and ego, street bravado and bullshit. And when she whispered to him, "Shhhh, baby . . . everything's gonna be all right," she made him break the most sacred promise to himself . . . as he wept for her.

eleven

The days of waiting had been interminable. But now her family had gathered to escort her to the hospital and she'd gone into preop, practically signing away her life with all those waivers—Teri hovering over the paperwork like a guard dog, and her husband clutching her hand.

Although she'd taken the preoperative cocktail and had an IV stuck in her arm, she didn't feel the least bit relaxed, as the nurse had promised.

Maybe it was the stricken look on Lem's face when it was time for her to be wheeled down the hall into this freezing room with bright lights. Or maybe it was because she was invaded by an uncomfortable catheter, and another tube forced oxygen through her nose.

Her body was no longer her own, it was *theirs*. Strangers had it. Strangers moved about it. Strangers talked about her in the third person. She was just meat on a table, and they were going to cut her, invade her, go into her and possibly take away the most sacred part of her womanhood. She needed to sob, but couldn't.

A mask covered her face, and she followed the anesthesiologist's orders to breathe deeply but normally, and to count back from one hundred. Her doctor looked like he was wearing black night-vision goggles, like he was a Green Beret paratrooper, to invade her sacred territory.

He smiled at her from behind his hospital mask.

Bird closed her eyes and drifted on the sensation of floating. She wondered if her mother felt this light, this disembodied, when she'd finally let go and drifted up to God?

It was becoming hard to keep her prayer vigil going. Thoughts and sentences fractured and drifted off into quick flashes of memory. She struggled to go over all the things she'd done before today. Her will was in place; Teri had seen to that. She'd told everybody how much she loved them. She'd apologized for things she'd done, and even things she didn't remember, but maybe they did. She'd gone to church last Sunday, so hopefully her house was in order.

Her arm felt a gentle touch. People's voices were becoming muffled. A lazy sensation of peace claimed her. These were some good drugs. She felt that gentle touch again, from a remote part inside her. Her eyes opened inside her mind. The light around her was bright. Her mother was smiling.

Her mother was talking to her without moving her mouth. She could talk back to her mom the same way. It was as though they could hear each other's thoughts. "I miss you so much, too," she told the dear face beside her. "And I'm so scared."

"You did good, baby," her mother's voice told her. "You were strong for everybody this week, and they needed that, even more than you did. It took courage, baby girl of mine. I love you. I'm proud of you. Momma's not going anywhere."

A whimper escaped her lips. "Momma . . ."

A male voice answered her. "Bird, honey."

A soft touch landed on her face, a kiss brushed her forehead.

Voices came into range, chasing away the floating feeling, and sending her mother away. She wanted to sob. Why did they send her mom away again?

"Easy, baby," the male voice soothed.

She concentrated hard on the task of opening her eyes. Deep, blurry brown hovered just above her face. Lem!

As she recognized him, awareness slammed back into her consciousness. She squeezed his hand, trying to use that same telepathy to ask for all the answers she needed immediately. Was she whole?

"Everything is gonna be all right, baby," his voice quavered, and he brushed her forehead again with a kiss.

Frustration to know more made her struggle to speak. Was she *whole!*

"Am I . . ." God, her throat hurt and her mouth was dry and sticky.

"Well, I see our favorite girl is coming around," another male voice said. "You were under for a very long time, Mrs. Van Adams, and are going to be sore for a few weeks—but we got everything out."

She shut her eyes against the horror of what the doctor had just said. *They got everything out.*

"No, baby," her husband rushed in, picking up on her terror as her nails dug into his palm. "They didn't have to do the hysterectomy, and got all the fibroids."

"You'll be fine. You'll need to stay here for a day or two, and then you can go home. The discharge nurse will be in to go over all the home-care procedures with you and your husband, but for now, we want you to stay in postop recovery for a while longer to monitor you. Once you're moved into your room, all your family can come visit."

She was still a little sore as she leaned over to put on a pair of pantyhose. But she would not be moved. Lem *had* to do this.

"Bird, you are so stubborn," he fussed, fiddling with the knot in his tie. "This is not important. It's a dead subject, so why you keep insisting that we all have to go over to the Center is beyond me."

"You're wasting time," she said in a pleasant tone, slowly standing and hoisting up her hose.

"Look at you, though, baby. You're still tender, moving a little slow. If we had to do this, it coulda waited. You don't have to prove some point. I already got my prayer answered."

She kissed him as she passed him, ignoring his protest, and went over to the closet to slip on a dress. "This okay?" She held the bronze-colored dress out for him to approve. "You think with my brown heels, and my clutch?"

His wife was the most exasperating woman on the planet—but he was glad she was on the planet, and back to her old stubborn self. "Yeah, that's fine. You'll look great in that," he said gently and went over to kiss her.

When they arrived at the Community Development Center, Teri was already there, early as usual. Lem scanned the boardroom as he and Bird entered it, noting that Teri was grilling Iola Carter and the legal coach, Linda Maxwell. Russell Hampton left the circle and walked over to Lem and Bird, extending his hand to Lem.

"Whew!" Russell said with a low chuckle. "Glad you're here." He gestured in Teri's direction, as he shook Bird's hand. "Got a tough audience in the house tonight, Mr. Van Adams. And I thought the banks were bad."

Lem smiled. If Russell only knew.

"But it's worth it." Bird squeezed Lem's arm as she left to join Teri and the other instructors.

He hoped Bird was right. Lem's gaze followed his wife's form as she sashayed away.

"The others will be here soon, right? Pulaski is on his way over, too. He'll help field any questions about the designs. But the rest of your family are coming, aren't they?"

"Yeah, don't worry," Lem told Russell. "My brother and sister-in-law are always late."

The group of women, which now included his wife, made their way over to him and Russell.

Iola Carter greeted Lem with a wide grin, and her eyes sparkled with mischief as she gave him a sly, discreet wink. Oh, yeah, she'd been given a Teri Joseph workover—but it appeared the sister could hang.

To his surprise, Teri hugged him quickly. Lem returned the gesture, a little stunned. Teri wasn't big on hugging people, least of all him. Maybe things had cooled out somewhat, but it was still too early to tell. However, Linda Maxwell had an expression on her face that ranged somewhere between ready to fight and glad to see him. Teri was a piece of work.

"You know, Lem," Teri quipped, glancing at the legal coach. "Linda and I have worked together before—on different sides of the table, but she is a rather good attorney."

"Thank you for the endorsement," Linda Maxwell said with an exhausted tone.

"I took the liberty of calling Ashland's office," Teri said, making the faces in the small circle blanch.

"Seems he's hired my fired paralegal full time to answer his telephones. Wendy Schultz had to go, after we got wind that she was leaking confidential client information to Ashland—but that's another issue. The point is, Lem, I informed him that you would not be needing his services, because you were firmly entrenched with family representation, and had the Community Development Corporation's coaching team at your disposal. Hope you don't mind?"

He wasn't sure what to do with that. Part of him

wanted to snatch Teri by her neck for getting into his business, and for being so thoroughly presumptuous. The other half of him took her stepping in as an endorsement to remain in the family fold. He saw the brief tension in Bird's face, and relaxed. Yes, the Joseph sisters were at it again—but it was all good.

"That's cool, Teri," he said. No more static, no more arguments, no more wasting time on petty nonsense—that had been his promise, if God gave him back his wife in one piece. "I'd better get up to the front and get ready to do this."

"Let me help you," Iola Carter offered.

He could tell that the sister would have given her eyeteeth to get out of the battering conversation she must have been having with Teri. He found it amusing as Linda Maxwell delicately extricated herself from Teri as well, feigning a reason to help set up the technology that they both knew Linda didn't know how to operate. Russell took it upon himself to act busy as the host, finding pads of paper and pens, anything, it seemed, to get away from Teri. Lem smiled. She wasn't that bad. You just had to get used to her complex way.

Lem chuckled inwardly. Everybody couldn't be wrong. His sister-in-law was definitely a trip, but he'd learned to appreciate the fact that the harder she pressed, the more it meant she cared.

By the time Kenny and Maxine arrived, all in a big huff and puff, he was set up at the front of the room, Bird was chatting away at the table with her sister, and the coaching team seemed relaxed. Bruce Pulaski had joined them and was talking a mile a minute with the other instructors. This was good. But the one person he was really concerned about was his boy, Kenny. How was Kenny going to react to all of this?

They really hadn't talked about the argument that they'd had. Once Bird's health situation had arisen, none of that seemed important. Their discussions had centered on logistics; was he coming in to work, how many days did he need to be out, arrangements for Jay, and Bird's recovery progress. Just the facts, no real talk.

Maxine had been the same way, focused on the tasks at hand to keep the family businesses and schedules flowing. She'd been the one to take care of Jay and get him back and forth to Mrs. Jenkins. Max was the one who brought plates of food and cooked up huge Tupperware containers of dinners. She also managed the calls and carried out Bird's instructions at the salon until Bird could get back—routing Bird's clients to the other stylists, and demanding that Bird heed the doctor's advice to do only a few hours on her feet at first. What would they have done without Maxine?

His sister-in-law's smile warmed him as she approached him with Kenny in tow, and began taking off her coat. He could only hope that the family peacemaker was going to be at her best tonight, because her husband's expression and mood were hard to read.

"Hey, Lem," Kenny said without emotion, extending his fist for Lem to pound.

But his brother-in-law hung back, didn't give him a fast embrace. Cool, he could dig it. All this had to be hard to swallow for Kenny. But Maxine had smiled at him and came in close for her customary hug.

"We are all so proud of you," she whispered, giving him a peck on the cheek. "Knock 'em dead."

Lem nodded, and used Maxine's good vibes as his cue to move toward the podium. It was now or never. No sense in prolonging the inevitable. The financing would be a question that he no longer cared about. It was still hanging in the balance for the banks to deliver a verdict on. But whether this project flew or not wasn't the issue. What was important was for the family to understand what he'd been trying to do.

Lem nervously took his position at the front of the room once everyone sat down and got settled in. At his graduation, he knew what he was going to say, had rehearsed it a thousand times. Even a room of fifty people hadn't made him so tense. But this was family. This was different. He truly cared what they thought, and more important, it was critical that they understand that this is what he'd spent his time on—not doing something shady. He had to let them know that it was just a dream, not something that he would allow to jeopardize his wife or his son, and that he'd long since given up on even considering using her salon to back this. The only reason he was here was because Bird had insisted. She'd been the one who wanted the whole family to know what he was capable of, and that was the only reason he'd agreed.

But now, standing in the front of the room, every opening line, everything he'd thought he'd say to them, evaporated. The blue light from the Power

Point projector held him in a temporary trance. Why had he let her talk him into this? It was a bad idea. Definitely a bad idea.

"I have something to say, before Lem does," Bird said, standing up and pushing away from the long table.

He could only stare at her as she came to the front of the room. He yielded the walnut podium to her, half thankful that she was up there, and half afraid that she might say something to cause a lot of emotion to erupt before he had to address the group. Bird was unpredictable—all of the Joseph women were.

"I wanted my family to come out tonight so they could see what I see in Lem Van Adams. I wanted you all to see what a person can do when he believes in himself, and when others suspend judgment to allow him to become the best he can be."

She paused and touched his arm. Her gentle smile reinforced him.

"He kept this a secret because he wasn't sure how the family would react, or how I would react—and none of us took well his attempt to do something else on his own. I can only speak for me, but I didn't know where he was or what he was doing, and I thought the worst of him. I was wrong. And that had to hurt." She gazed at him with love and commitment.

"And sure," Bird continued, "he could have told us about it early on, and we can all say—after the fact—that we would have been supportive. But I'm not so sure that's completely true. My husband wanted to see if he could do this for himself first, then drape it on everybody . . . and all he asked was for some space to figure it out alone, before we all jumped in and started adding our two cents."

Bird's gaze went to Teri's and held it. "I also don't want any of you thinking that Lem, or I, are asking for any financial support from anybody. We are here because we wanted to make sure nobody thought there was anything shaky or secretive going on. That's the reason I pushed Lem to do this presentation tonight—that's right, *I pushed him,* and not the other way around. So don't get any kooky ideas that he manipulated me while I was sick. I know how y'all think."

Bird chuckled as Teri smiled and Maxine joined her. Even Kenny had to offer a begrudging half smile.

God, he loved this woman. How did she just get it all, from the fragments he'd been saying all along, and despite all that she'd been through? Bird leaned up and kissed him, and he felt ten feet tall.

"Give him a chance, y'all," Bird insisted. "Just give him a chance, hear the man out, and then we'll all go from there."

His wife stepped away from the podium, and Iola Carter headed to the front of the room. He could only assume that the women had quietly strategized on his behalf. This was too choreographed to be a coincidence. But this time he was glad that they'd done so. They had his back. He smiled. Bird was up to her old tricks, and oddly, he appreciated that she was.

"May I speak for just a moment?"

Lem nodded and let Iola have center stage. They

were warming up the crowd, walking point for him, and confidence began to kindle within him. It threaded through his bloodstream as Iola talked about the need for family support of entrepreneurs, and as she gave the history of the organization. He knew that this part of her speech was designed for Teri and Kenny—the boss and the foundation.

The boss would want credibility to factor in, would want to be sure that the people he was dealing with were on the up-and-up. Kenny would need to be convinced of why this idea had intrinsic family value, how it would help the whole, and make the community a better place for all the children in the clan and neighborhood one day. He'd want a philosophical underpinning to this endeavor, whereas the boss would want to be sure that it could in no way jeopardize her sister. Iola Carter was a master. But Bird was incomparable.

Lem finally took his position when Iola yielded the floor, and he stated his case with conviction buttressed by the truth. Words became more than words; they became an impassioned argument, statements of possibilities, and his vision for opportunity took fire within his brain again, fueled by his wife's eyes, which reflected her unconditional pride and support.

Russell Hampton was also on point, helping to explain the financial issues, and the brother was honest. He told everybody how far off this dream still was to becoming a reality, and how the banks would review the proposal—how they'd see it coming from a person with a past. And he appreciated how Russell subtly weaved in a philosophical bent to the argument, explaining the rock-and-a-hard-place position of someone who was trying to make good after doing wrong.

Then Linda Maxwell chimed in from her legal perspective, fully outlining the Catch-22 that he'd been in. She walked back and forth in front of the long table as though she were addressing a jurors' box—and perhaps, in many ways, she was. But she delivered her closing arguments with gusto, and spared no opportunity to give the project praise.

And Pulaski was Pulaski, bringing the enthusiasm of youth to the group, firing them up while waving his hands before the white boards. His naïveté about the obstacles facing a man with a record, and his unwillingness to allow that to undermine his belief system, actually seemed to underscore the point—a man had a right to dream.

Iola Carter closed the case, spreading an impressive array of letters from significant corporations out on the table. It was clear that her goal was to show the group, especially Teri, that others believed in his project. And without saying it directly, she implied, why couldn't his family?

Lem paced himself, allowing questions to rise from the family and handling them as they came. Nothing rattled him, oddly. He'd emotionally distanced himself from this project, because whether it flew or not no longer seemed to matter. What mattered most was the beautiful, petite woman beaming at him with pride. What mattered was that she'd wanted him to do this, wanted to show him off to the family, as though he were her prized possession. And his instructors had reacted the same way. So, the outcome didn't matter.

The gift in this evening was that he'd been given his chance to say his piece, and his family had listened respectfully while he did so. No matter what else went down, he'd always have this night as a jewel to savor forever. Bird had given him this.

"So, that's what Bird and I wanted to show you all. Any questions?"

Dead silence.

Now he was nervous again. This was not the Joseph-Chadway style.

His instructors looked around the table, and glanced at everyone's faces. Not a peep. All eyes fell on Teri. She shook her head. *Teri didn't have anything to say?*

"Well, all right then," Lem said nervously, clicking off the blue light of the projector with the remote. "I guess that's all I had to say."

Silence.

It took a moment to process that Kenny was slowly rising to his feet. Lem's stomach clenched. Damn. The brother was so disgusted that he was just going to get up and walk out without a word? He knew Kenny could be rough on people when pissed, but *man*— Lem let his breath out hard and looked down, trying to accept the disappointment that was beginning to seep into him.

So be it. He'd tried.

A low clap made him look up. Kenny's huge hands were striking each other in a slow, emphatic cadence of approval. His eyes held Lem's gaze, and his hands began to move faster. Maxine shot up from her chair and was on her feet, as was Bird. Teri took her time, but obviously found it in her heart to stand and clap, too. Bird rushed up to him, and her arms were hugging him. His instructors were standing now as well, clapping, too. Acceptance flowed from the group to surround him and his wife.

It was all a matter of perspective.

"Baby, you asleep?" Bird whispered, raising herself on one elbow to peer down at him in the dark.

"No, just thinking 'bout tonight."

He felt a kiss on his chest and he gently pressed his wife's head down onto his shoulder. Feeling her relax against him gave him a delirious sensation of peace.

"You were so good tonight," she whispered. "Thank you."

"No, baby. Thank you. I couldn't have done it, or gotten them all there, without you. It meant a lot to me, Bird. Thank you for having my back."

"Of course I've got your back, silly. Did you see the look on my sister's face?" Bird giggled and he chuckled with her. "I have never in all my born days seen Teri rendered speechless."

"I think that was only 'cause she'd blown her load grilling my instructors before we got there. Girlfriend was just temporarily out of ammo. By tomorrow, she'll be packin' again."

"I know," Bird said, giggling. "But I also know my

sister well enough to know when she's impressed. Teri was blown away."

"You think so?" The thought was totally satisfying, and he was glad his wife had shared the morsel of information, popping it into his consciousness for him to savor. Success was indeed sweet.

"Brother," Bird exclaimed, "You rocked the house!"

He laughed. His wife was such a nut.

"It was good, wasn't it? I mean, my instructors really held court in there."

"All y'all did," Bird said, leaning down to kiss him, "but you were the best."

"Think Kenny was really okay with all this?"

His wife pulled back and gave him a quizzical look. "Are you kidding? You know Kenny ain't one to front. If he had a problem, he'd be the main loudmouth in there, talking about how this or that didn't make sense. Then he'd be standing up, or rearing back in his chair to deliver one of his state-of-the-world-according-to-Kenny speeches."

Lem laughed harder. What Bird said was too true. "Then it's all good."

"Yeah, it is," she whispered, her voice taking a sexy turn that stirred him.

When she kissed him again, her mouth lingered. He gently pulled back and looked up at her, stroking her hair as he spoke. "We still only have the yellow light, baby. I miss you, too, but I don't want to hurt you, okay? We'll wait for the green light from the doctor."

She pouted, and then smiled. Her gaze was tender. "You're right."

She let out her acceptance in a long, frustrated sigh that messed with him. He was glad that she wanted him, but wasn't even going there.

"Time is going real slow for this light to turn."

He chuckled. "Bird, stop."

He saw her face go from playful to crestfallen, and then suddenly realized something from the past—*talk to her*.

"Baby," he murmured as he turned her over easy on her back. "I miss you so much I can't hardly stand it. But I never, *ever*, want to hurt you. Okay? So, baby, stop. Please."

"You're feeling it, too, a little bit, huh?"

That was the stone cold truth. He wanted her so badly it didn't make sense. "Yeah, and you know that, so stop messin' with me like this, Bird." He chuckled.

Wow. She smiled, vindicated. This wasn't like before—he wasn't rejecting her. He was just worried, but still horny. God bless him—he loved her that much. She could tell by his intense look, and by what he'd said, that the six weeks were killing him, too. That's all she wanted, though: a little indication that what had happened after she'd been injured in the car accident wasn't happening again. She wanted to be sure that he still found her appealing, after all he'd seen and all the doctors had done and said. They weren't even thirty yet . . . a man just had to understand some things like that. But the look on his face gave her a sense of triumph. All right, she was satisfied.

"Okay. Two more weeks. I understand."

"No, you don't," he warned with a chuckle.

"Oh . . . yes, I do," she murmured.

"Baby, stop. The voice thing you're doing is killing me. *No, you don't.*"

She laughed and he laughed with her. Her body relaxed. She leaned over and kissed him. He dropped beside her and rolled over on his back, then slung his arm over his eyes again, and groaned.

"No, you don't," he insisted.

"Ohhh . . . yes I do."

She traced his chest with her finger. He turned over on his side to give her his back and she spooned him. He groaned again. She sighed peacefully and began drifting off in the comfort of their closeness. For better or for worse . . .

Yeah, it was all good.

twelve

"It is my turn to cook, Maxine, so I don't know why you won't quit it. I'm fine now, and it's time to get things back to normal." Bird let out a sigh of exasperation as her sister fussed over the phone about how it might be too soon for her to resume the Sunday dinner rotation.

"Well, we could all just eat at your house. Teri and I could bring all the food over, and stay to wash up dishes, since Lem's clocking extra hours with Kenny to help with the backlog," Maxine went on in a cheerful voice. "But you are just so damn stubborn, Bird. Always have to have your way, ever since you were a baby."

"*I'm* stubborn?"

"Yes. Stubborn. Would throw a hissy fit if any of us wore a blouse of yours, or used your barrettes. God help anybody who borrowed something without asking—so don't try to act like you don't have your ways, Bird. You are a trip." Maxine laughed hard into the receiver. "And, girl, you know we can help on that cooking thing. Whew, child!"

"I am not a trip, Maxine. And I am not as bad a cook as everyone makes me out to be. Lem likes my cooking just fine. So just because I know what's my due, and you all are encroaching upon my turn at—"

"See, listen to you. This is just what Teri and I have always had to put up with. Poor Lem."

Bird laughed. "Leave my poor husband out of it. You're the one who just won't back off. I told you, I'm fine. I have a clean bill of health, for goodness sakes, Max. And, besides, we went over this during the week. Everything was all settled on who was bringing what, and I already have a turkey in the oven—so just bring your butt on over here with the stuff you were supposed to make. Okay? Jeez, Louise, you sound like Lem."

Both sisters laughed as Maxine conceded.

"A turkey," Maxine sighed. "Ambitious, kiddo. But I'll bring plenty of gravy, just in case."

"Max, you know you are not right!" Bird laughed harder at her sister's truthful comment. "Plus, I prayed over the turkey—maybe God'll have mercy on it."

"Make plenty of iced tea," Maxine wheezed through pants of laughter. "At least my brother-in-law is over there keeping an eye on you. *And* making sure you behave—Lord knows, none of the rest of us can."

Bird chuckled as she peeked into the oven to check on her turkey, pleased that it was browning nicely. "Your brother-in-law is getting on my nerves, girl—like you. He's been tiptoeing around me like I'm a piece of glass, or something."

"Ohhh, really." Maxine's warm voice filled the receiver and coated Bird's ear with mirth. "Scared he might break it, huh?"

"Max!" Bird replied, shooing her sister away with her hand, even though Maxine couldn't see it. "He's just nervous, is all—he thinks he might hurt me."

"Give him time, sweetie. He'll come around. I remember Kenny acted like that after every baby. Even though the doctor said things were fine, he was still all eeeky, and whatnot. Scared to really get loose, if you know what I mean, as though what he had was bigger than his kids' heads. Girl, pullleease, you know men are crazy."

They both laughed hard, and Bird sat down in a kitchen chair. She loved talking to her sisters. Had missed the simple joy of their kitchen conferences, the ones not marred by high drama or tragedy. Maxine always had a bit of mother wisdom to impart, and made her feel better.

"They are crazy, aren't they?"

"Totally," Max agreed.

"Speaking of crazy, have you talked to Teri this morning? I noticed she wasn't in church again. I wonder what that means?"

"If I know our sister, it means she was either sleeping in, working out, or at work on some legal brief."

Bird sighed. "Think she and Damon will make it? Maybe hook up for good, this time?"

"See, now, you are going to have to ask Teri about that. I stay out of Ms. Teri Joseph's man business, and Bird, if you had any sense, you would, too."

Bird laughed as Maxine chuckled her warning.

"I just want her to be happy, too, Max. Like us."

"You are happy, aren't you, baby?" Maxine sighed. "I'm so glad."

Silence surrounded them like the soulful aromas that were wafting from her stove through the house. Yes, she was happy. No—better than that, contented. It was a warm feeling like the butter than ran over the tops of biscuits, something to savor and roll around on one's palate. Bird sighed.

"I know that sigh." Maxine issued one right back. "Yeah, honey, when everything is going right all at the same time."

"Uhmmm, hmmm." Bird closed her eyes and leaned her head back against the kitchen wall, thinking about Lem. "And that's what I want Teri to have, too."

"Didn't you hear anything Rev said today about letting go and letting God? Girl, you better stay outta our sister's business before you ruin your own peace and get caught up in some mess again."

"Oh, Max." Bird couldn't help but laugh.

"Oh, Max, nothing, girl. See, I know what your problem is."

"Now, just what is my problem, Maxine?" She *loved* teasing her older sister. There was just something so delightful in making Maxine become peevish.

"Your problem is that you have excess energy. So, you better find a way to get Lem to come around, and handle *your* bizness, child."

"Well, I guess you would know, since you have my brother-in-law reading love sonnets to you in bed." Bird laughed hard now, glee making her pop up from her chair as Maxine cranked up for a good-natured fair one.

"Oh, now, heifer, I'm getting off the telephone. Don't you even *think* about hinting to Kenny that I told you some stuff I shouldn't have told either one of y'all—you hear?"

"I'm not gonna mess up your groove, Max. Besides, *we're* not thinking 'bout y'all. You ought to be thanking your brother-in-law for your recently hot bedroom, girl. Be glad somebody got in your business."

Maxine's gasp made Bird double over as she howled with laughter.

"Bird, Bird, get back on this phone this minute and stop laughing! What did you tell Lem about my business? Oooh, girl, wait till I get to your house."

"Bye."

"Bye, hell, hussy. Tell me."

"All I said was that Kenny was acting all stodgy and whatnot, and I told Lem that women like to hear romantic things. So, since we couldn't do anything else, I read him one of your poems, and—"

"You did not! Oh, Lord, Bird. Not one of the more . . . uh . . ."

"Hot ones? You mean, one of those ones about how it feels when you are aching for the familiar touch—"

"I am getting off the telephone to come over there—with my sneakers on, my hair pulled back, and Vaseline on my face and no earrings!"

"Oh, Maxine, you have such a way with words, girl. My husband loved it. So I just suggested that he tell Kenny to—"

"I'm gonna hurt you, Bird. I'm gonna hurt you bad when I get over there."

Again, they both laughed. Bird shook her head as she walked back to the stove.

"I love you, too, Sis. See you in a little while."

"Be down in a minute, baby," Lem hollered in a rush, coming through the door and hurdling the stairs two at a time to head for the shower. "Sorry I'm late; house smells great. Tow job was a monster. Snow was a bear to maneuver in. Y'all save me a seat. Hi, Teri."

"Hey, Lem," Teri yelled back from the kitchen.

"Hurry up, baby," Bird chimed behind Teri's greeting. "Glad you're home in time."

He jumped in and out of the water as fast as he could. Although Bird had said it would be all right for him to help Kenny with the work that was backed up at the garage, he didn't want to leave everything on her shoulders for the dinner. As he'd dashed into the house, though, everything seemed to be in control. Bird was handling it, so he'd catch the cleanup on the back end. That was cool.

The doorbell sounded below as he swiftly pulled on his jeans and sweater. He was hungry, and from the smell of things, Bird definitely had some good eats waiting. Maybe her sisters had finally transferred Momma Joseph's skills to her.

Somehow, he'd grown to appreciate the Sunday get-togethers. The chaos didn't rattle his nerves like it used to—and he was glad that Bird had fought everyone tooth and nail to put their home back into rotation again.

"Yo, Kenny," he yelled, bounding down the steps. Issuing hugs to the clan all around, he slapped Ahmad five, kissed Kelly, brushed his youngest niece's forehead with a kiss, and scooped up Jay from the floor so that his son could kiss his giant-sized uncle, tall aunt, and cousins.

"Thanks for puttin' in the hours today," Kenny said. "Whooo-wee, something sure smells good! Bird outdid herself, seems to me. Smells like Thanksgiving all over again in here, man."

"Yeah, it does," Lem agreed, kissing Maxine, who held a baby on one hip and a pan on the other.

"Hi, Lem. Everybody else in the kitchen?"

"Yeah, Sis. Teri's back there working Bird's nerves about her turkey, and Bird is arguing with her to leave her alone. I hit the shower, trying to stay out of the middle of it."

"Wise man," Maxine replied, handing her youngest daughter to Kenny as she headed toward the kitchen without taking off her coat. "I have my own score to settle with Miss Bird, myself. Best you men stay in here out of harm's way."

Kenny and Lem watched Maxine disappear into the kitchen.

"I ain't touching that, brother," Lem said, shaking his head.

"You know what it's about?"

"Naw, bro. Stay out of it, if you know like I know."

The men sat down on the sofa with the two

youngest children on their laps, advising Ahmad and Kelly to stay put and to be in the safest place possible—in front of the television with them.

Lem bounced Jay on his lap, trying to keep his son occupied while Kelly and Ahmad began fighting over the shows they'd watch.

"Hey, hey, hey, that ain't no toy, y'all," Kenny boomed. "Put the game back on, too, while you're at it."

Lem stifled a chuckle. His brother-in-law was as predictable as clockwork. The man would never change, but he loved him.

"How's the financing moving along on your building, man?"

The question came out of the blue as Kenny set his daughter down in a depression in the cushions between him and Lem, steadying the baby with a gentle push to keep her from toppling over. Deep.

"Going good, man. Real good. The jury's still out, but they haven't said no, either. So that's positive—as much as I can hope for right now."

"Good. That's good."

"Maybe one day, when you got some time, maybe you could come over and take a walk through—I know you're crazy-busy and all, but I'd like you to see it. Not like it's ready or anything, it will take months if all the financing comes through . . . and that's a big if. But I just thought you'd like to see what I was trying to do. The actual building, not just a presentation."

"That'd be good, man. I'll make time to do that."

"Cool."

"Cool," Kenny repeated, and pounded Lem's fist.

Why couldn't conversations with women be this simple? Basic. Bottom line. No drama. Just say what you gotta say, clear the air, and move on. They must have been thinking the same thing, for their gazes traveled away from the game on TV and went to the sonic boom of female shrieks and laughter coming from the kitchen.

"Lem, man, why can't it just be simple, no static?"

"I don't know, man. If I figure that out, I'm gonna go on Oprah and get fat-paid. You feel me?"

"I hear you, man. Why does it have to be all of that?"

"You gentlemen ready to eat yet?" Maxine strode out of the kitchen with a wide grin, balancing a hot pan of candied yams above pot holders.

"Are you kidding?" Kenny stood and picked up his daughter. "Was waiting for y'all to stop yakking and get the show on the road."

Maxine rolled her eyes at him and sucked her teeth, then ordered them all to wash their hands as she walked away. Only Kenny could get away with saying some mess like that. Lem knew better than to even go there with Bird. He stifled a chuckle as he gathered up Jay, and shooed Kelly and Ahmad to go wash their hands. Kenny was already in the dining room, getting his daughter into a high chair.

"And where is my kiss?" Bird asked with a pout as she passed by Lem with a succulent-looking turkey on a platter surrounded by stuffing.

"Right here, baby," he murmured, sweeping her

mouth and following the food. "Y'all was in there burning, for real, for real."

"Like I wasn't," Teri fussed, coming up behind him with a steaming bowl of string beans in one hand and a basket of cornbread muffins in the other.

"Oh, no," Lem offered, half meaning it and half just trying to keep the peace. "I know you were back there keeping things together."

"That's right," Teri said, pecking his cheek as her sisters went back to bring out more food. "Table looks nice, Bird," she hollered, receiving a "thank you" yelled back from Bird.

Lem got Jay into his high chair, then he and Kenny waited for the women to enter the room. As they came in he stood behind his normal chair, to Kenny's right. But something was off. People were all confused and bunched up. It was simple—all they had to do was sit down.

"You're in my seat," Kenny said with a sly grin. "I've been in yours here lately, it seems."

Lem studied Kenny's expression for a moment. He couldn't believe it as Kenny moved away from the head of the table and stood behind the chair that Lem normally occupied.

"Seems I've been misseated, too," Teri said, nudging Bird with her elbow to take the seat at the foot of the table.

A bewildered look came over Bird's face as she slowly rounded the table and took what was always Teri's seat. Lem could dig it; he was just as confused as Bird was. Deep.

"Well," Maxine said, "now that things have been put to right, can we all sit down and eat?"

The noisy process of people settling in didn't distract Lem from holding his wife's gaze. He could tell that she hadn't orchestrated this; her sisters and Kenny had. That it came from them meant more to him than any of them would ever know.

"You gonna bless the food, brother, so we can eat?"

Lem stared. Kenny was giving up grace, too? Very deep.

"Er, uh, I suppose so," Lem stammered, trying to collect his thoughts.

"Oh, Lem, now don't act like you can't talk in public, or something," Maxine fussed. "Pullease, Reverend Van Adams, you just need to stop with the bashful act."

"Maxine, would you shut up and let the man just bless the food," Teri scolded through a wide smile. "My goodness."

"C'mon, Reverend Van Adams. We're all hungry. Get your preach on, so we can chow down." Kenny gave Lem a broad grin as he spoke.

"We both have a lot to be thankful for," Bird said softly, her gaze holding Lem's.

"The food is getting cold, people," Kenny reminded them, breaking Lem's trance with his wife, and making them all laugh.

"We do have a lot to be thankful for," Lem agreed, as the family members joined hands in preparation for the prayer. "We all do indeed."

Visit the
Simon & Schuster Web site:
www.SimonSays.com

and sign up for our
mystery e-mail updates!

Keep up on the latest
new releases, author appearances,
news, chats, special offers, and more!
We'll deliver the information
right to your inbox — if it's new,
you'll know about it.

SIMON & SCHUSTER
A VIACOM COMPANY
www.SimonSays.com

POCKET BOOKS

SONNET BOOKS